Francesca Scanacapra w
and Italian father, and her
England and Italy. Her adul
she has pursued an eclectic
working as a technical translator between Italian, English, Spanish and French, a gym owner in Spain, an estate agent in France, a property developer in France and Senegal, and a teacher. Francesca lives in Dorset and currently works as a builder with her husband. She has two children. *Paradiso* is her first novel and the first of the *Paradiso Novels*.

Paradiso

Francesca Scanacapra

SILVERTAIL BOOKS • *London*

First published in Great Britain by Silvertail Books in 2021
www.silvertailbooks.com

978-1-913727-06-2

For Nonno Mario, Nonna Franca and Zia Rosa,
whose spirits and stories inhabit this novel.

CHAPTER 1

Pieve Santa Clara, Lombardy, 23 October 1944

I was woken early on the morning of my departure by the shrill jingling of a bicycle bell and the scattering of gravel in the yard. I leapt from my bed and threw open the window to see a young priest rapping hard on our door.

'The road is clear!' he called. 'Get to the meeting point within the hour!' Without waiting for a reply, he hooked his leg over the saddle and made off at speed, the tails of his cassock flailing behind him.

'Within the hour?' exclaimed my mother. 'Graziella, quick, get ready!'

I was dressed in more clothes than I knew I possessed and bundled into the kitchen. My parents tried to coax me to eat, but I could not swallow a thing.

'You'll be back home soon, my little one,' said my father as my mother hurriedly buttoned my coat.

Hugging my father could not be done spontaneously. I always had to announce my intentions so that he could position himself comfortably, but that morning I flung my arms around him without warning and gripped him hard. He winced and let out a low moan, then he held me for a long time, kissing my head more times than I could count.

My father was the most important person in my life. Of course I loved my mother, and I loved her very much, but I loved my father more.

'Please, Graziella,' said my mother, pulling me from my father's arms. 'Be a good girl. We have to go.'

A pale winter sun was starting to break through the morning mist as my mother and I set off towards the village. She was walking so fast I had to trot to keep up. Even my feet were layered with extra clothing. Two pairs of stockings with socks on top made my boots far too tight. I hobbled, dragged along by my mother, and wondered what sort of a place I could be going to that would be so cold.

'Mamma?'

'What is it?'

'Will I have to wear socks and stockings all the time?'

'No, just for the journey. It's easier to wear clothes than to carry them.'

As we approached the village we joined other groups of mothers and children hurrying towards the piazza. They appeared from all directions, hand-in-hand and carrying scruffy, hastily-packed belongings. I don't know what I had been expecting, but I was not prepared for the chaos of humanity who clustered around several open-backed trucks parked in the square.

'Who are those people?' I asked my mother, gripping her hand.

'They're from other villages,' she replied.

It had not occurred to me before that moment that the village of Pieve Santa Clara was not the only one being evacuated. I clung to my mother as we joined the haphazard line. More queued behind us, pushing us forward into the heaving crush of bundles and overcoats. The smell of damp wool, unwashed people and clothes filled my nostrils. The crying and calling of children and mothers filled my ears. Panic rose through me.

'Don't send me away,' I begged. 'I don't want to go.'

My mother looked down at me and for the briefest moment I thought she might concede, but instead she shook her head and said, 'You have to be safe and away from the soldiers.' And with a thin, unconvincing smile, she added, 'Just think how many new friends you will make.'

'I don't want new friends! I want to stay with you!'

My mother crouched down so that our faces were at the same level. 'This is just a precaution, Graziella,' she said.

'What's a precaution?'

'It's something you do just to be extra safe.' Her tone was gentle, but grave.

'But what will happen to you here? What if the soldiers come again, or if one of the bombs hits our house? How will I know if you're killed?' I held my breath so I wouldn't cry.

'Everything will be all right,' she said. 'Be a good girl and everything will be all right.' But she didn't sound as though she meant it.

'How long do I have to go for?'

'I don't know. Just until it's safe to come back. Nobody knows how long the war will last, but it can't go on for ever.'

I hung my head and stood rooted to the ground, trembling. The prospect of being entrusted to the care of strangers for an indeterminate time froze fear deep into my bones. Despite my state of over-dress, my hands were so cold that they hurt.

We were shoved and jostled forwards. Dozens of children had already been loaded into the trucks. Some were pale and grim-faced. Others were flushed and crying. Some just sat wrapped in blankets with their heads bowed.

More children were being processed by a woman with a moustache. As each family approached her, a few words and paperwork were exchanged. Swift goodbyes were encouraged, but children and mothers would not let go. Every final hug and kiss led to another final hug and kiss.

My mother's grip on my hand became tighter and tighter as we edged our way towards the moustached woman.

'Your child's name?' she asked.

'Graziella Ponti.'

The woman traced her finger down a list of names and nodded.

'She will be going to the Convent of the Blessed Virgin near Lodano in the province of Pistoia. I need her ration card, please.'

My mother hesitated. 'Can she not keep it with her?' she asked.

'No. It will be kept together with those belonging to the other children and given to the sisters.'

When my mother protested, the woman was adamant. It seemed she had had the same argument with every mother there.

'We cannot take her unless we have her card,' she said firmly. 'And we need to get going soon, Signora, whilst the road is still clear.'

Reluctantly, my mother relinquished the card.

'Thank you, Signora. Please sign here.'

My mother did as requested.

'Am I going a long way away?' I asked.

'Far enough for you to be safe,' replied the moustached woman. 'Take a blanket and go to the blue truck.'

My mother wrapped me in her arms and pressed her face hard against mine.

'Be good,' she repeated. 'Be a good girl and everything will be all right.'

'Signora, we need to get moving,' said the lorry driver. He was a craggy old man with half a damp, spit-infused cigarillo hanging from his mouth. He peeled me from my mother, took me in his arms and lifted me into the back of the truck. His soil-stained, callused hands grasped me with a gentle strength, as though I weighed nothing at all.

'Go as far to the front as you can and sit down,' he said. 'No standing during the journey.'

As the lorry horn blasted there was a frantic rush of activity and noise. I looked at my mother for one last time before more children were loaded on and I was shunted forwards and lost sight of her. A moment later the tailgate was closed and the lorry juddered into life. I had never seen as many little girls as were crammed into the back of the truck. I recognised some from church, but the rest were unfamiliar to me. As I lived outside the centre of the village and had not yet been to school, I did not know many children

I was seven years old. I couldn't remember a time without war, but it had meant little to me before then. My existence had revolved around the sheltered confines of family and home. Despite our poverty, my life was serene. But the brutality of war fought not on battlefields, but in the streets of my little village, had been condensed into three days of horror where my world had been shattered.

*

My only playmates in Pieve Santa Clara were my cousin Ernesto and my friend Rita Pozzetti.

Rita was my age. We were born just a month apart. Our fathers, who were lifelong friends, had also been born just a month apart. Rita and her family lived on the other side of the road. I played with her whenever I could, but she was a sickly child, frequently stricken with bronchitis, coughs and fevers. Most of my time was spent with my Ernesto.

Ernesto was five years older than me. He was my aunt, Zia Mina's, son. Zia Mina had been married to my father's older brother, but he had died when Ernesto was very young. My own father attempted to provide some paternal influence, but Ernesto did not like rules, or restrictions, or doing as he was told. My father used to say that one boy like Ernesto was enough for ten fathers, but ten fathers would never be enough for one boy like Ernesto.

I joined in his boyish games, making camps in the hedges, chasing rabbits and digging for worms with which to lure toads. He said he didn't mind the fact that I was a girl, and for my part, I quickly learned not to be precious. In fact, I was more than happy to clamber and scramble, caked in mud or soaked in water from the stream which bordered the garden. The fields and woodlands around our home were our playground, where we could wander and ramble at will.

Ernesto could climb almost any tree with the speed and agility of a cat. Of all the trees in our garden, his favourite was the ancient chestnut tree which grew beside the house.

My father had hung a swing from one of its branches, but Ernesto soon grew bored of its intended use. Rather than swinging, he would climb one of the long ropes. It was the only way he could access the lowest boughs of the chestnut tree. Once he had scaled the rope he would clamber up to the very top of the tree, branch by branch. Seeing him balanced precariously so high up in the canopy made my aunt frantic. She would try every possible inducement and threat to get him back down, but Ernesto would just laugh.

We could be quarrelsome companions. Our difference in age and stature meant that he could out-fox and out-run me. He would taunt me by kidnapping my dolls and sprinting away to hide them in the branches of trees, where he knew I had no chance of retrieving them. My mother had chased him from the house with her broomstick when she caught him trying to put a frog in my bed, but despite his maddening tricks, I loved Ernesto.

Two days before my departure, my mother and I had been preparing to walk my father to the village when Ernesto sprang into the kitchen and asked, 'Can I come with you?'

'As long as you behave,' my mother warned him. 'And don't run off.'

'I'll be an angel, Zia Teresa.' He grinned, stretching out his arms and fluttering his fingers.

Mamma raised an eyebrow then said, 'All right then. There's bound to be an enormously long queue for the shop. You can keep a place in the line for me while we go to the cemetery.'

'All right,' replied Ernesto.

'Go and tell your Mamma then, and ask her if there's anything she needs. And put something warm on.'

Ernesto was never cold. He had bounded into the kitchen barefoot. One winter's morning my aunt had woken to find him building a snowman in the garden, still dressed in his nightshirt. She fretted constantly that he would catch his death, but he never did. He seemed miraculously immune to the cold and to illness.

He disappeared for a moment, then reappeared pulling on his yellow knitted waistcoat.

'Mamma wants me to see if there's any sugar today,' he said.

'If there is, don't eat it on the way home.'

Ernesto laughed. 'I wouldn't do that, Zia Teresa.'

My mother tutted. It was exactly what Ernesto had done two weeks previously. My aunt had been furious, but he had charmed her into forgiving him. Charming his way out of trouble was something at which Ernesto was highly skilled.

We walked down the road towards the village hand-in-hand, following my parents. Ernesto was complaining about his waistcoat.

'It's itchy,' he said, scratching at the nape of his neck. 'And hot. And it's yellow. Yellow's not for boys.'

My mother gave a disapproving look over her shoulder. 'You're lucky to have it,' she told him. 'Stop grumbling.'

There was nothing extraordinary about the scene in the village that morning. People were going about their daily business. Women with children and shopping baskets congregated to chat in the piazza. Several old men sat outside the bar playing cards, reading newspapers and smoking cigarettes. The line of hopeful customers outside the shop crept along at a snail's pace. Ernesto joined them.

'Make sure you stay in line,' said my mother sternly. 'Behave yourself and don't wander off.'

Ernesto grinned cheekily and fluttered his fingers again.

I wanted to stay with him, but my mother wouldn't let me. Despite his assurances, Ernesto couldn't be trusted not to stray. A friendly dog, the thought of a climbable tree, or an instant of boredom were enough to divert his attention. We had disappeared many times before when Ernesto had been distracted. My mother said she had no wish to search the length and breadth of the village for us.

We carried on without him. We didn't have far to go but progress was slow as my father, despite having my mother's support on one side and a stick on the other, needed frequent rests and occasional sips from his bottle of medicine. As we rounded the corner of the road which led to the cemetery he stopped to catch his breath. It was then that four armoured German vehicles rumbled past.

Until that moment I had seen remarkably little military activity. Occasionally, Italian soldiers passed along the road in front of our house. I was allowed to wave at Italians and had learned to recognise their uniforms, but if German soldiers passed I would be ushered inside quickly.

My father had told me that Germans had no business being in Italy and that the Italian soldiers were fighting to make them leave, but the Italian army did not have enough men, so soldiers from other countries such as England and America were coming to help.

I had been in the garden with Ernesto one day when we heard a thunderous booming in the sky.

'Look!' he shouted. ' Aeroplanes! American aeroplanes!'

We had never seen aeroplanes before. Ernesto stood transfixed, gazing upwards and thrilled at the sight, while I, who knew that aeroplanes carried bombs, ran to hide in the barn and remained concealed under a wheelbarrow until I was sure they had passed.

Short bursts of gunfire in the distance were common. They came from near the railway line, and my father said that they were just warning shots, fired to signal to the trains that they should stop. I had grown so used to them that I paid them little attention.

However, that morning, there was a prolonged burst of shooting which came from the direction of the piazza.

'Oh my God – Ernesto!' exclaimed my mother, letting go of my father, but he grabbed her and held her back.

'Stay here,' he commanded.

'But Ernesto's down there!'

'He's quick and smart enough to hide. You can't go down there, Teresa. You don't know what you might walk into.'

Neither of my parents looked at me. They stood immobile, ashen-faced, staring at each other.

The gunfire rattled for several long minutes, then stopped. My father still held on to my mother.

'Go back home across the fields,' he told her at last. 'Take Graziella and stay out of sight. I'll go and find Ernesto and bring him home.'

My mother opened her mouth to object, but my father insisted.

'Go,' he ordered. 'Go now! And when you get home, go inside, close the shutters and bolt the doors. Tell Mina to do the same.'

My mother took my hand and ran with me. The fields were cloaked in fog and wet with dew, which soaked our skirts and boots. We climbed over fences and through hedges, sharp grass cutting the skin on our arms, and brambles and thorns snagging our stockings.

Zia Mina had heard the gunfire. She was standing at the gate watching for our return, but we did not arrive via the road. We clambered into her vegetable garden through the shrubbery, our clothing and hair woven with twigs and leaves.

'What's happened? Where's Ernesto? Who's shooting?' she said. Panic shook through her voice.

My mother told her she didn't know, but the two women did

as my father had instructed. They pulled the shutters closed and locked us in. It was then that our windowpanes were rattled by a further burst of gunfire. I stood in the corner in silence in the darkened kitchen, my wet boots still on my feet.

We waited. My mother and my aunt paced the floor and said little. There was no more shooting, but it was over two hours before we heard the creak of the gate outside and my father's voice calling to be let in.

'Thank God!' cried my aunt, clasping her hands together and raising her eyes heavenwards.

As my mother slid open the bolts my father stumbled in, drenched in sweat and gasping for air. Ernesto was slung across his shoulders. My father staggered to the table and let the boy tumble from his grasp. He landed with a dull thud on the wooden top.

I was seized by my mother, who screamed and pulled me away, covering my eyes with her hands. I heard my aunt howl as Mamma clutched me tightly and buried my face in her apron.

My world was blind and muffled, but as I felt my mother's body tremble, fear infected me. I didn't know what had happened, but Mamma never cried, so I knew that it must be something terrible.

'I want to see,' I said at last. 'Please, Mamma.'

'Let her,' I heard my father's voice say. 'She needs to understand.'

My mother released me slowly.

I was aware of the smell before anything else – a butcher's shop aroma, like cut meat. It crept into my nostrils and I could taste it in my throat.

Ernesto lay spread across the kitchen table. I stared at him for a long time, waiting for him to move, but he did not.

I edged forwards, still holding onto my mother's skirt, until my face was level with the table top. Ernesto's head was twisted towards me. His eyes were open and I looked into them, but they did not look back at me. He was an odd colour. A bluish tinge had coloured his mouth. His yellow waistcoat was soaked red. It took me a while to understand that he was dead.

My aunt stood trembling, gripping the edge of the table and staring at her son. She was as pale as he was. Each wailing breath left her body in a series of stuttering gulps.

'Who did this?' she sobbed. 'Who did this, Luigi?'

My father had collapsed on the floor. He could barely speak. 'Those bastard sons of whores,' he said at last.

Five boys from the village had managed to procure two shotguns and had lain in wait in the upstairs room of a house which overlooked the piazza. The company of German soldiers whose vehicles we had seen pass had parked in the square. The boys had opened fire on them. The surprised Germans had returned fire immediately, and five boys armed with two shotguns were no match for twelve soldiers with machine guns.

Pandemonium had erupted in the piazza. People had panicked and run for cover. Most had barricaded themselves into the church, but Ernesto had run in the direction of the cemetery, to join us, I thought. He was killed by a single German shot to his back and had lain in the road where he had fallen until my father found him.

Gradually the kitchen quietened and a heavy silence took hold. My mother and my aunt lifted Ernesto's body and carried it away. The only thing my mother said to me was, 'Stay here and help your Papá.'

My father's face and clothing were encrusted with Ernesto's blood. His hair was matted against his head. I helped him out of his jacket and saw that the blood had soaked through to his shirt.

I tried to get him to his feet, but he could not stand. He yelped and sucked air through his clenched teeth.

'Fetch me a chair,' he gasped. 'The sturdy one.'

11

Bracing himself, clinging to the chair with what little strength he had, he heaved himself up and limped over to the sink, dragging the chair behind him. Then he lowered himself sideways onto the seat and stripped off his stained shirt.

My father could not bathe without assistance. I had watched my mother help him to wash countless times, but I had never washed him myself. I tried to soap a washcloth, but the water was cold and the soap would not dissolve.

'Shall I heat some water, Papá?' I asked.

'No. Just do what you can,' he replied hoarsely. He gripped the edge of the sink and rested his head on his hands. His bony shoulders shuddered as the cold water touched his body, and I saw how his bent spine pushed up through his skin.

*

All news spreads quickly in a village, but news of death spreads with the greatest speed. My father was barely dressed when Rita's mother appeared carrying a large basket covered with a cloth. My friend's father, Luigi Pozzetti, was a carpenter and therefore the one called upon to make coffins. As a result he was also the undertaker, but he had left the village to go to war years before. During his absence the task of preparing the dead had been left to Rita's mother, Ada Pozzetti.

I was only allowed to go to my aunt's part of the house once Ernesto had been washed, dressed in his Sunday clothes and laid out on his bed. His eyes and mouth had been closed and his hands folded across his chest. The meaty smell of the fresh bullet wound had gone, replaced by the spiced scent of carbolic soap and camphor.

Candles were rationed and we only had a few stubs between us, so my aunt lit oiled rags in jars which filled the room with a brownish fug.

A priest arrived sometime later. He delivered the rites and spoke about the dead going to heaven, just as Christ had done. I thought of the fresco in the church above the altar which depicted Jesus ascending to a turquoise heaven surrounded by angels and imagined Ernesto doing the same, fluttering his fingers and grinning.

I kept my gaze fixed on Ernesto, waiting for the moment his body would rise towards heaven, but he remained dead still as the priest anointed him with oil and holy water. Tiny droplets fused together and slowly trickled down his cheeks.

'Is he crying?' I asked, but nobody answered my question.

Zia Mina's grief took the form of an eerie calm. As soon as the priest left, she said that she needed to be alone with her son.

My mother prepared a supper of bread and broth, but none of us could eat. The table had been scrubbed clean of blood, leaving a dark shadow of dampened wood and the smell of vinegar where Ernesto had lain. The pot sat untouched in the centre of the stain until it was cold. I was put to bed early that night.

'Luigi, what happened to those boys?' I heard my mother say.

'The bastard Germans stormed the house,' he said. I could hear the rasp of tears in his voice again. 'The boys were trapped upstairs. They didn't stand a chance.'

'Did they kill them?'

'Not right there and then. They brought them down to the piazza, made everybody come out of the church, then lined the boys up and shot them in full view. They left the bodies on the church steps for everyone to see. They were such young boys, Teresa. No older than fourteen and every one of them had lost a father, or an uncle, or a brother.'

There was a moment of silence, broken by my mother's dismal wail.

'But Ernesto? Why did they kill him too?'

'He must have been running to find us,' said my father quietly. 'If only he'd gone into the church with the others.'

'Oh God, it's all my fault! Why did I let him come with us? Why did I leave him in the square? And I could have left Graziella there too. I almost did. It could have been her too!'

'Teresa, you couldn't have known. Nobody could have known. Do you think that if I had had even the slightest inkling of what was about to happen I would have let you and Graziella walk to the village with me? Nobody knew what those boys were planning. I don't expect even their mothers knew. It's not your fault. None of this is your fault.'

I could hear my mother weeping as she cleared away our untouched supper. Her words rang through my head. What if she *had* left me in the queue? Would I have run for cover in the church, or would I have followed Ernesto?

'What were they thinking?' my father said heavily. 'What did they expect? Five foolish young boys with revenge and misguided ideas of heroism in their heads.'

'What will happen now?'

'It's going to bring trouble. The soldiers have already gone looking for their families. Word was sent as quickly as possible to give them time to hide, but the Germans are going from house to house looking for them and for other boys.'

'Are there more?'

'Who knows? How do you prove your boy isn't a would-be Partisan?'

'Do you think they'll come searching here?'

'I expect so.'

'Mina shouldn't be alone. She could come face to face with the very soldier who killed Ernesto.' My mother's words became choked with tears. 'Oh Luigi, how could this happen to a good woman like Mina? She's lost everybody. Everybody! How could this happen?'

As the words left my mother's lips, there was a pounding at the door and a shout from outside.

'Oh God in heaven!' I heard her cry out.

'It's all right,' my father comforted her. 'We have nothing to hide. Try to stay calm.'

I heard him heave himself out of his chair and go to unbolt the door. A German voice spoke curtly in heavily accented Italian.

'Boy?' said the voice. 'You have boy?'

'No. Just a little girl,' replied my father quietly.

I gripped my covers and held my breath as brisk, heavy-booted footsteps crossed the kitchen and approached the bedroom. The door was pushed open, but the light from the kitchen was blocked by the figure of a gigantic man. His shoulders were as square as the doorframe and he had to duck his head to come in. He stepped inside and poked at my parents' bed with the barrel of his rifle. Once he had satisfied himself that it was empty, he looked underneath it, then one by one opened the three drawers of the clothes chest.

Our small bedroom was shared, but I had a bed of my own. It was a wooden blanket box in which I had slept since I was a baby. My father had removed the lid for fear I would accidentally shut myself in and suffocate. It had a warm, comforting smell of starched linen and laundered sheets, but suddenly that night my bed seemed frightfully cold.

The enormous German soldier peered down at me. I should have pretended to be asleep, but instead I stared at him, wide-eyed. Terror paralysed me. A glint of light from the kitchen bounced off the muzzle of his gun. He slipped his hand down the side of the box and felt underneath me, then nodded and said, '*Geh schlafen!*'

I didn't know what it meant, but I snapped my eyes shut and he left.

My mother came into the room, stroked my hair and told me everything was all right, but I knew that was far from true.

My father followed the soldiers through to my aunt's part of

15

the house. They shouted at him to stay back, but I heard him say, 'What threat am I to you? I'm an unarmed cripple, for God's sake!'

They shouted again and I heard the clicking of guns being cocked.

'Luigi!' screamed my mother, pushing me down under my blankets. 'Luigi, for the love of God don't make them angry!'

My aunt opened her door before the soldiers had time to knock. They asked the same question they had to my own parents.

'Boy? You have boy?'

My aunt nodded and quietly led them upstairs to where Ernesto lay.

'There,' she said. 'There's my boy. And may you be damned for what you have done and burn in hell for eternity, you bastard sons of whores.'

She spoke the words so calmly in her soft Cremonese dialect that the soldiers did not understand their meaning. Perhaps they did not realise their involvement in Ernesto's death. There was nothing to suggest that Ernesto had died violently, or at their hands. He was just a dead boy.

The soldiers removed their hats and nodded condolences at my aunt. She nodded her acceptance in return and gestured towards her kitchen table, where several bottles of her home-made liqueur sat ready for visitors, as was customary following a bereavement.

The soldiers needed little encouragement and took a glass each, then called out to the other soldiers who were standing in the yard waiting for them to complete their searches. They filled my aunt's kitchen, clinking their glasses, laughing and smacking their lips. My aunt's liqueurs were famously delicious and the soldiers complimented her in broken Italian.

'*Buono! Buono!*' They cheered loudly as they banged their glasses on the table for more, seemingly having forgotten that there was a dead child in the room above them. By their fourth and fifth glass they were red-faced and thoroughly stewed.

They didn't thank my aunt. They flung their chairs back and left, taking with them all six bottles from the table. I watched as they crossed the yard, singing and passing the bottles between them. They didn't bother to search the barn or any of the outbuildings. We could have been hiding an army of resistance fighters and they would never have known.

At some point during the night the clattering of a machine gun reverberated in the distance, making my mother toss and mutter in her bed. I couldn't sleep. My only thoughts were of Ernesto. I wanted to see him one last time before he went to heaven.

I slipped out of bed, wrapped myself in my mother's shawl and crept through to my aunt's, where I tiptoed up the stairs and into Ernesto's room. The oiled rags had burned out, leaving only a smell of seared fat and singed cloth. I peered through the dim shadows and looked to see if Ernesto was still there. He was. He was lying in my aunt's arms.

'Graziella?'

'Yes, Zia Mina.'

'What are you doing here?'

'I wanted to see Ernesto.'

My aunt reached out her hand towards me. 'Come,' she said.

I sat beside her, cradled in one arm as she cradled Ernesto in the other and suddenly I was overcome with a terrible thought.

'Zia Mina, is Ernesto going to heaven?' I asked.

'Of course.'

'Even though he was naughty?'

My aunt said, 'God forgives children everything. He lets all His children into heaven.'

'When is he going then?'

'He's already there.'

'But he's still here.'

'His soul has gone to heaven. When we die we leave our bodies here on earth and our souls go to heaven. He's with his Papá now.'

'What's it like in heaven?'

'It's a garden filled with angels and light.'

'Are there lots of trees?'

'Of course.'

'Ernesto will like that.'

'He will.'

With my eyes closed I pictured Ernesto, not floating up to heaven like Jesus in church, but climbing an enormous chestnut tree, his sinewy arms and legs pulling him effortlessly skywards. He looked down at me, smiled, waved and disappeared into the canopy of leaves. It was not long before I was asleep.

I must have slept very deeply as when I awoke I was in my own bed and had no recollection of how I had made my way back there. As I stirred, I was aware of voices in the kitchen, talking in urgent whispers. I sat up, trying to make out who was there.

My parents, Rita's mother and an old man were standing around the table. Their conversation stopped as soon as they saw me appear at the door, and the old man took his leave.

'Come here, little one,' said my father, beckoning me over. Everybody's gaze followed me. My father took my hands in his and looked at me gravely.

'We need you to promise us something,' he began. 'We need you to promise that you will not tell *anyone* that the German soldiers came to our house last night. You must not tell anyone they were here, or at Zia Mina's. If anyone asks you, deny it. Even if it's somebody you know, do *not* tell them. It's very important. Nobody must know. Nobody.'

My father squeezed my hands.

'I would never tell you to lie, my little one, but this is very, very, very important. Do you understand?'

I was forbidden from playing outside in view of the road that day. My parents told me to stay where they could see me and not to venture out of the vegetable garden, but there was little for me to do without Ernesto's company. I sat on the swing, looking up into the branches of the chestnut tree. If I closed my eyes tightly and opened them again suddenly I thought I could see him for a fraction of a second.

Once I had grown bored of the swing I moved to the kitchen step and sat quietly, trying to play with my dolls, but I was too distracted to invent a game. All I could do was turn them over and over in my hands.

I was very fortunate to have dolls. My mother was highly skilled with a needle and thread and had made them from scraps of fabric too small to be useful for clothing. They had ruby red embroidered lips, huge green eyes and woollen hair. One had a damaged arm from where Ernesto had wedged her in a branch. My mother had repaired the tear, which looked like a long scar.

People came and went from Zia Mina's house throughout the day to offer their condolences. A coffin was brought over from Rita's. The old man who had been in the kitchen that morning returned later in the day to speak to my parents. I was told to stay outside. As he was leaving he spotted me. I had been peering through the window.

'Did you see German soldiers here last night?' he asked.

'No,' I replied, swallowing hard to steady my voice. 'They didn't come to my house.'

'Good girl,' he said, pinched my cheek and left.

Later in the day my mother went to a meeting. When she returned, the first thing she said to my father was, 'We have to send Graziella away.'

My father was silent. I felt fear tighten my body.

'Are you sure?' he replied after a long time.

'Yes. It's not safe here now.'

'Where would they take her?'

'To a convent up in the north. There will be less risk up there.'

My father let out a long, low whistle.

'They said there could be hundreds of Germans here within a couple of days, perhaps even sooner,' continued my mother. 'Eventually they will realise that some of their men are missing and questions will be asked.'

'How many of them were killed in the end?'

'Twelve.'

'Twelve? Good God! Are they all buried now?'

'Yes.'

'Where?'

'They won't say. The fewer people who know, the better.'

'And Mina's bottles?'

'Smashed and buried elsewhere.'

'How long do they reckon we've got?'

'A day or two at best. That's why we have to send Graziella away. It's not just because of what happened yesterday. They said the Allied bombings are going to intensify. They're going to hit the bridges and the railway lines. We're too close for comfort, Luigi. We have to get our daughter away while we still can.'

'What has this world come to?' my father lamented. 'All this devastation, all this death, all this hunger all over again.'

'We have to do the best we can. At least we can be grateful that you're not part of it.'

I gave little thought at the time to the buried Germans, or the smashed bottles, or the fact that I had been told to keep a secret. Even Ernesto's death seemed secondary. My head was filled with the fear of being sent away. I had never been out of the village before, and I had certainly never been away from my family.

My mother busied herself preparing my belongings.

'Is Rita going away too?' I asked.

'No.'

'Why not?'

'She has a bad chest.'

'I wish I had a bad chest.'

My mother looked up from her packing, but said nothing.

'Can I take my dollies?'

'You don't have much room. Remember that you have to carry everything yourself.'

'Please, Mamma,' I begged.

My mother considered this for a moment. 'Perhaps you could take just one.'

I looked at my dollies carefully. 'I want Rita to have the other one then,' I decided. 'I don't want her to forget me.'

My mother smiled at me. 'That would be a nice thing to do.'

My farewell to Rita was brief. My mother was in a hurry and she told me not to sit too close for fear I would catch my friend's cough. Rita was looking flushed. Her eyes were bloodshot.

'Where are you going?' she croaked.

'To a convent.'

'Will there be soldiers there?'

'Mamma says no.'

'I wish I was going. I was so scared when they came here last night. Were you scared?'

'The soldiers didn't come to my house,' I said quietly.

It was then that Rita was overwhelmed by a fit of coughing. She sat up and spat great globs of green phlegm into a bowl by her bedside. My mother ushered me away quickly, covering my nose and mouth with her hand.

I left one of my dollies at the foot of Rita's bed and promised to think of her every day. I kept the dolly with the scarred arm.

CHAPTER 2

As I sat huddled in the truck clutching my doll, the shock of the previous days hit me hard. I had not cried when I had said goodbye to my mother, and nor had she. We had exhausted our tears. I felt tired, frightened and empty.

The lorry headed north out of Pieve Santa Clara. We had been told to remain seated, but I knew that we would soon pass my house and I felt compelled to look, just in case it was the last time I would ever see it; just in case I became lost amongst the crowds of displaced children and nobody knew where I should be returned to once the war was over; just in case during my absence everything I knew should disappear.

I pulled myself up, gripping the high side of the lorry, and was able to catch the briefest glimpse of home before a pothole jerked me back down to the floor. With my knees drawn up under my chin, I closed my eyes and prayed that I would be back soon, even though I had barely left.

I knew nothing of other places. The only countryside I knew was the Lombardy Plain – a flat, agricultural landscape where maize, wheat, linseed and even tobacco grew in abundance.

To me, the fields were endless. No matter how far from home Ernesto and I roamed, wandering between rows of crops, or following the furrows left by the ploughs, there were always more fields stretching out beyond. Sometimes we trekked as far as the boundaries of the rice fields, where we would climb the banks and throw stones into the shallows to spook the herons. The huge birds could reach up to a metre in height with wing spans almost twice that. Their size frightened me, but Ernesto was bigger and braver than I was. He would lie in wait, then leap to his feet in a burst of noise, causing the birds to panic and take to the sky. Their screeching was so loud that I would have to cover my ears.

The rice fields were flooded knee-deep during growing season, but we knew to keep out of the water. It was full of leeches and water-snakes.

In the lorry, a girl in a pink hat was sitting beside me, rummaging through the contents of her bundle with the panicked air of someone who has mislaid something precious. I watched for a while as her fumbling grew more frenzied, until at last she let out a gasp of relief.

The object of her search turned out to be a photograph, which she kissed. Before I could ask who it was, she turned to me and said, 'It's my father. He sent it all the way from Sicily.'

The picture was of a man in military uniform, but it was taken from a distance. It could have been anybody.

'Where's your father?' she asked.

'He's at home.'

'What's he doing at home? Why isn't he saving our country?'

'He has a bad back.'

The girl in the pink hat frowned, as though trying to decide whether a bad back was simply an excuse for cowardice.

'Will he go and fight when he's better?' she asked.

'He won't get better,' I replied.

'Was he hurt in the war?'

I shook my head, feeling that if I began to speak aloud my tears would start, and if they did I was not certain I would be able to stop them.

My father would never be fit to fight in a war. His battles were of a different kind.

The girl in the pink hat continued gazing at the photograph and in that moment I wished more than anything that I too had a photograph of my father, even one taken from a distance. It would be easy to recognise him. He stood twisted, stooped and pigeon-toed. At the age of thirty he had the posture of a very old man – but it had not always been the case.

My father had been a skilled mason. In the spring of 1940 he was cranking a winch to haul a load of bricks onto a scaffolding tower to perform a repair on the church belfry when one of the wooden trusses splintered and gave way, causing the scaffold to collapse and the cradle of bricks to fall and crush him under its weight. My father suffered a broken leg and pelvis, and permanent damage to his back.

Most people agreed that he was lucky to have escaped with his life, although luck seemed to touch him very infrequently after that day. Before his accident he could run up a ladder with a stack of a dozen bricks on his shoulder and a full bucket of cement in his hand. The aftermath left him barely able to walk.

My father had been a hard-working young man with dreams and plans for his family's future. It was not just his body which the accident crushed. It was presumed that he would never work again. However, a few weeks before my departure my mother had told me that we were expecting an important visit from Don Ambrogio, the parish priest, and that the reason for his house-call was the possibility of a job for my father.

I attempted to ask questions whilst my mother washed my face and hands in preparation for the visit, but she said, 'Just sit quietly whilst Don Ambrogio's here. Let Mamma and Papá do the talking.'

'Will I be able to have some cake?'

'Yes. But only if you sit quietly.'

My mother had been saving her sugar and wheat-flour rations and had prepared a small quantity of cake mixture, just one egg's worth, which she had taken down to the village at five o'clock in the morning for the baker to bake in his oven. It was early autumn and the weather had not yet turned, so our stove was not lit. In any case, wood was being saved as it was rationed.

She had waited in the shop during the entire time her cake was baking for fear that somebody would steal it. Rationing drove honest people to do dishonest things. My father would say that opportunity could make even the most moral man a thief.

The cake sat on the sideboard, cooling under a handkerchief, its scent wafting so temptingly around the kitchen that it made my stomach rumble. I was forbidden to touch it under any circumstances. Even lifting the handkerchief to peek or sniff at it was not allowed.

My mother opened the door as soon as she heard the creak of the gate outside. I watched from the window as two priests made their way across the yard, strutting like a pair of crows.

'Welcome. Please come in. Do take a seat,' said my mother, smoothing out her dress.

'Thank you, Signora Ponti. You are most kind.'

Don Ambrogio looked over to my father who was sitting by the stove with a hand braced on each knee. It was the only position in which he could control his spasms.

'My apologies if I don't stand to greet you, Don Ambrogio,' he said, his hands tightening on his knees. 'It takes me a while to stand.'

'No apology necessary, Signor Ponti. It is a miracle you are here at all, seated or standing.'

Don Ambrogio pulled up a chair. He was large man, whose flaccid chins spilled over his collar. He smelled of sweat, wine and mothballs. The second priest was in every way his opposite. He was thin-lipped and hollow-faced with a hooked nose as sharp as an axe.

'May I introduce you to Don Gervaso?' said Don Ambrogio, gesturing graciously towards the second priest. 'Don Gervaso is charged with the parish of San Martino, where he is involved in the most generous and munificent charitable work with cripples and mental incompetents, as well as those wounded by the Great War.'

Don Gervaso bowed his head humbly.

'We fear that there will be many more wounded who will require the same care as a result of the current war,' mused Don Ambrogio. 'We can only pray that peace will return swiftly.'

Don Gervaso nodded in grim, tacit agreement and took a pencil and a small black book from somewhere in the folds of his cassock.

I sat silently on my stool, as instructed. Neither priest seemed to notice I was there.

'Could I offer you some refreshment?' asked my mother, smoothing out her dress again. 'I have a little chicory if you would like that.'

Rationing had made coffee a distant memory, so mixtures of barley and chicory and anything else dark brown in colour were used as substitutes, albeit very poor ones. Even the addition of black sugar made from beets did not make it any more palatable. According to my father, it was like drinking a mixture of mud and cow piss.

'You are very kind, Signora Ponti, but Don Gervaso has to return to his duties at San Martino very shortly, therefore much as we would like to, we will not be able to tarry long. Although, is that the aroma of sponge cake I can detect?'

'Yes, Don Ambrogio. Only a very small sponge cake, of course, but you are welcome to have some.'

Don Ambrogio clasped his doughy pink hands together. His fat lips glistened with saliva.

'How delicious!' he exclaimed, sniffing the air. 'Perhaps you would permit me to take a small sliver home with me?'

'Certainly,' said my mother. 'And for you, Don Gervaso?'

The other priest raised his hand in polite refusal.

'Don Gervaso has undertaken not to consume anything which might be considered a luxury whilst we are in the grips of war,' explained Don Ambrogio. 'He has even relinquished all but the most basic of provisions from his ration card.'

Hearing this pleased me very much. If I was a good girl and continued to sit quietly, Don Gervaso's slice of cake might be for me.

Both priests turned towards my father, and Don Ambrogio began his questioning.

'Signor Ponti, you say you have trouble standing. How mobile are you?'

'Once I am standing I am quite mobile,' said my father. This was not exactly true.

'Would you consider yourself robust enough to undertake some light physical work?' Don Ambrogio continued. 'Work such as sweeping, or weeding, or perhaps whitewashing a wall?'

My father considered this a moment and nodded.

'Yes. I am improving daily and I'm sure the more I move, the less stiff I will feel.'

'Could we trouble you to show us the extent of your mobility, Signor Ponti? Perhaps you could stand?'

My father shifted his weight uneasily in his chair. My mother was at his side in an instant and offered her arm in support. My father heaved himself to an upright, albeit crooked position.

'Are you able to raise your arms above your head, Signor Ponti?'

My father obliged.

'Excellent! And are you able to bend down to retrieve something from the ground?'

'As long as it's not heavy,' said my father, at which point his back gave a spasm, making him jolt.

'Are you all right, Signor Ponti?'

'Quite all right, thank you. I have a little cramp, that's all.'

Don Ambrogio took a cup of flowers, which my mother had placed on the table in honour of the visit, and set it on the floor at his feet.

'Do your injuries allow you to stoop to pick up this small object?' he asked.

My father stepped stiffly towards him. The two priests watched him intently. Don Gervaso's pencil was poised above his notepad.

Slowly and deliberately, and with a thinly-disguised grimace, my father bent his knees and squatted down. He took the little cup delicately between his fingers, raised himself to a standing position and placed it back on the table. I knew he felt pain, but he did not show it.

The two priests nodded. Don Gervaso wrote something in his book.

'Do you require a stick to walk?' was Don Ambrogio's next question.

'Only if I have to walk a long way.'

'A long way being how far, would you say, Signor Ponti?'

I looked over at my mother, whose lips were pursed so tightly they had almost disappeared. My father had attempted to walk to the village just the week before. He had turned back after 200 metres and staggered home, only to collapse by the gate. My parents did not tell the priests this.

'I walk every day, and each time I try to walk a little further than the previous day,' my father said lightly. 'Without a doubt, I am improving. A distance which seems a challenge today will be like a pleasurable stroll in no time at all.'

'Excellent, Signor Ponti! I admire your spirit and determination. Sometimes God tests us in ways we cannot begin to comprehend, but through those trials He allows us to develop qualities which otherwise may have been unknown to us.'

My father rubbed his hip. I could see that he needed to sit down.

'Indeed,' he said, sounding unconvinced.

Don Ambrogio turned to Don Gervaso, bowed his head towards him and muttered a few words before turning back to my father and announcing, 'Signor Ponti. I, with the assistance of Don Gervaso's charitable organisation, would be delighted to offer you the custodianship, supervision and maintenance of the cemetery of Pieve Santa Clara. Don Gervaso's charitable organisation will supply funds to ensure you a salary. It will not be much, you must understand, Signor Ponti, but it will be something. And something is better than nothing at all.'

'I may need to take rests initially,' said my father, suddenly appearing overwhelmed at the prospect.

'Signor Ponti, nobody will be behind you brandishing a bull whip, I can assure you. Don Gervaso's organisation wholly understands the limitations of all those who require its help, as do I. ' The priest cleared his throat before adding, 'Of course, you cannot expect payment for days when you find yourself incapacitated, or if you are unable to work due to inclement weather.'

There was a moment of silence, broken by a sob from my mother. My father and the two priests turned towards her.

'Thank you. Thank you so much,' she said in a cracked voice. 'My prayers have been answered.'

Don Ambrogio made a sign of the cross and smiled. 'Dear Signora, what else is the Church for, if not to help its flock in their hour of need?'

My father was to be paid 100 lire for each full day of work. The average income for a labourer in those days was around 300 lire, but my father was not an average labourer. He was a broken-bodied man with little hope of any paid work. As Don Ambrogio had said, 100 lire was indeed better than nothing at all.

I had sat obediently on my stool by the window throughout the visit and not said a word, just as my mother had instructed. I felt a sense of excitement that at last my father could work again, but momentous though it was, my anticipation at the prospect of cake was greater.

My mother took her tiny cake from the sideboard and placed it in the centre of the table. It was smaller than the saucer on which it sat.

'I can wrap a slice in paper if you wish to take it home,' she offered, addressing Don Ambrogio. 'Are you sure you would not like some too, Don Gervaso?'

Once again, the other priest raised his hand in polite refusal.

'In that case,' said Don Ambrogio, licking his bottom lip as he eyed the minuscule cake, 'perhaps you would allow me to take a second slice? There are children in the village who have not tasted cake for over three years.'

My mother hesitated for a moment then said, 'Maybe you should take all of it, Don Ambrogio. A single slice will not feed many little mouths. Once you have shared it among the children, all I ask is that you return my cake tin.'

'Dear, kind Signora,' he said, and crossed himself again. 'I am overwhelmed by your generosity. May God bless you and your wonderful family.'

I watched in hungry, disappointed silence as the two priests left with my mother's cake. I cannot be sure how many children, if any, were fed – but the tin was never returned.

As soon as they had gone, my mother turned to my father and said, 'Is it going to be too much for you, Luigi?'

My father shrugged. 'We can't afford to turn down 100 lire, can we?'

A less indigent or more fainthearted man would have declined the priests' offer. Despite having been able to show that he could stand, raise his arms and lift a teacup, my father was in no condition to work. The physical agony that he endured was unremitting. No matter how carefully he moved, pain would immobilise him and he would whistle the air in through his teeth until his spasms subsided.

However, with a mixture of the spirit and determination that Don Ambrogio had mentioned, he had accepted the challenge of the work at the cemetery. At the very least, his salary would allow him to pay for his medication, which he was obliged to take in ever-increasing amounts. It was agreed that he would begin his new job the following day.

However, it was not just the work to be undertaken at the cemetery which was an ordeal. Getting there required walking a distance which my Papá had not managed since before his accident. My mother refused to let him go alone, so we went with him. It took us well over an hour to cover the single kilometre which separated our house from the cemetery. The walk exhausted my father. He slumped against the wall, pale and perspiring.

The cemetery had been neglected since the outbreak of the war. Tufts of grass and stringy weeds had grown over the paths. Since the government had begun its metal requisitioning campaign, railings and plaques had been removed. The entrance had previously been barred by a set of heavy iron gates and capped with a copper cross, but those too had been requisitioned. The gates had been replaced by a rudimentary barrier made of wood, and a rough cross fashioned from two planks.

'Are you sure you can do this?' my mother fretted.

'Of course. I'll be fine in a minute.'

'Do you want us to stay with you?'

'No, no. You go on home. I'll be gambolling like a spring lamb once I've caught my breath.'

We left my father at the cemetery. Retracing our steps took us barely twenty minutes. When we went to fetch him that evening we found him lying exhausted on the steps. He had drained the last of his medicine. The walk home took over two hours.

My father's boots, which had been wrecked as a result of his accident, would have cost at least 1,000 lire to replace – a sum that was so far beyond our means that they might as well have cost a million. My mother had fashioned a pair of shoes for him from canvas and made the soles from an old bicycle tyre, but they could not withstand the walks to and from the cemetery. They wore through after just three days, leaving my poor father's feet blistered and stone-lamed. My mother had enough rubber to replace one sole, but had to resort to layers of fabric and cardboard for the other, which made walking even more painful for him.

Somehow my aunt bartered a pair of sturdy leather boots for him. They were not new, of course, but were of good quality and had been used very little. I watched as my mother laced them up. My father walked twice around the kitchen table, grinning, then sat gazing at his booted feet for a long time, before inviting me to join him to admire them.

'I'm glad that someone else has gone to the trouble of wearing them in,' he said. 'Although I have never owned a pair of brand new boots myself, I have known men who have, and have been driven mad by the way they creak. These are just perfect. They have had most of the creak worn out of them.'

*

As the lorry drove along the straight flat roads of the Lombardy plains, so many thoughts of home were going through my mind that I had little notion of time passing. It was only when the terrain changed and began to rise that I was jolted back into reality.

The roads became rougher. Every bump and pothole jarred our backs and shook our little bones. Numerous children were sick and those unfortunate enough to be seated next to them were showered with vomit. I clutched my dolly and my small bundle on my lap, keeping them out of the way of the pool of sick on the floor, which oozed my way whenever we rounded a right-hand bend.

My possessions were stuffed into a rudimentary bag which my mother had created for me out of a piece of old apron. There were strict rules about what we could take. I had heard her complaining that it was not enough, hence the reason why I was so overdressed. We were allowed one change of clothing, a nightdress and slippers, if we had them, and very little else. My mother was right. It turned out to be a pitifully inadequate amount of clothing. I was grateful for my father's warm woollen socks, which made my boots so tight, but I could pull them up right over my knees, almost to the middle of my thighs.

The lorry laboured up winding roads, its gears grating before every corner. It spewed out smoke so thick it made us choke and left a greasy brown residue on our skins. It was probably a mercy that we were in an open lorry, or I am certain we would have been asphyxiated by the fumes.

We seemed to be climbing for a long time and as the inclines sharpened, we were all squashed back towards the tailgate.

A long-faced girl was talking to the girl in a pink hat.

'I saw them,' she said. 'I saw those boys laid out on the church steps. There was blood everywhere.'

'My nonna watched them being shot,' said the girl in the pink hat.

'There was another boy shot too.'

'The one lying in the road?'

'Yes.'

'He had nothing to do with it. They said he was just running away.'

I said nothing. I looked up at the sky and thought of Ernesto again. The light was fading; small windows of dim blue punctured the grey covering of clouds. I wondered whether he could see me. I thought of our last walk to the village, then of my father staggering home carrying his body. I pictured him lying dressed in his Sunday best in his darkened bedroom, of my aunt cradling him in her arms.

The sound of his voice repeated in my mind: 'I'll be an angel.'

'My mother said those German pigs got what they deserved,' said the girl in the pink hat, then she turned to me. 'Don't you think so?'

'The Germans didn't come to my house,' I replied, looking down at my doll.

'They came to mine. They pointed a gun at my brother. I'm glad they were poisoned after what they did. I hope they find out who poisoned them and give them a medal.'

The lorry ground to a halt. My whole body felt stiff and bruised. I had little idea of how long the journey took. All I knew was that it felt interminable and that nausea had given way to ravenous hunger. I had eaten little since Ernesto's death.

We were lifted out of the lorry one by one by the old driver, whose mushy cigarillo had dissolved into a brown stain in the corner of his mouth.

We looked all around, but we could not see a convent, or any building at all. We had simply reached the end of the road. A wave of panic surged through us. The girl in the pink hat grabbed my arm.

'They lied!' she shrieked. 'There's nothing here! They're just going to leave us here to die!'

A cacophony of screams and cries exploded into a frantic stampede as girls tried to clamber back into the truck. Somehow, amongst the hysteria of shoving and pushing, I managed to climb on too. I was elbowed, knocked over and squashed beneath a scramble of bodies. In the commotion I lost my bundle and my doll.

The driver was shouting and pulling back the girls who had not managed to get back into the lorry. They fought him, lashing out and screaming to be taken back home.

It was only the appearance of two nuns which finally calmed us. I was one of the first to see them. They came into view from behind a craggy outcrop, making their way down a rocky track. Seeing our distress, they assured us that we had not been abandoned – and we were instructed to follow them. We would have to walk the rest of the way as the only path which led to the convent was not suitable for a vehicle as large as the lorry.

One by one we were lifted back down. I found my bundle of possessions undamaged, but my dolly had been trampled on. Her good arm had been torn off and she had a footprint on her face. I stuffed her into my coat and joined the line of girls being assembled by the nuns.

The path which led to the convent was steep and made of shiny, step-worn stones. We picked our way through, following the nuns.

I had never seen mountains before. They seemed so dark and alien compared with my familiar landscape of flat fields and huge, open skies. There was a sharpness in the air, the unfamiliar smell of pinewoods and the echoing calls of birds which I did not recognise. Even the clouds seemed different. For the first time in my life I could not see the horizon.

It was made worse by the fact that I did not know which direction I was facing. I knew that we lived along the North Road, because it headed north out of Pieve Santa Clara. I knew that the village was south of our house. On a clear day I could see the top of the belfry. The sun rose in the east because I could watch it rise beyond Zia Mina's vegetable garden, and it set in the west, behind Rita's house. As I looked around there was nothing to indicate any cardinal point. It was a disorientating sensation.

As we rounded an enormous boulder, the Convent of the Blessed Virgin came into view.

The ancient building stood entirely alone, perched on a narrow plateau cut into the steep hillside. Its enormous fortress-like walls rose up three storeys. The few windows which pierced its outer confines were small and shuttered. A single slim bell-tower reached skywards.

Several more nuns stood outside to greet us, ruffling like blackbirds as the wind caught their habits.

We were herded through enormous front doors. My whole body was tight with dread. Nobody spoke. We were a stunned, shivering, moth-eaten gaggle of frightened little girls, stepping into an unknown world. However, the nuns fussed kindly, asking our names and promising us that we were finally safe.

'Welcome, girls, welcome,' they said cheerfully. 'Come in out of the cold.'

There was little discernible difference between the cold outside and the cold inside. As I stood in the cavernous entrance I felt a chill rise through the flagstones, bite through the soles of my boots, through my layers of stockings and socks and into my feet, which seemed to freeze instantly.

The convent walls were stained with mildew. The ceiling was a patchwork of bulging plaster, exposed bricks and shoddy repairs. There was a musty smell of stale lamp oil, mice and decay. Even when the colossal doors were closed behind us with an almighty, echoing bang, we could still feel the wind blowing.

I stood immobile clutching my bag and my doll, repeating my mother's words to myself.

'Everything will be all right. Be a good girl and everything will be all right.'

CHAPTER 3

Although everything around me was new, frequently unfathomable and often uncomfortable, I acclimatised reasonably well to life in the care of the sisters. We were treated firmly, but kindly. They kept us occupied and encouraged prayer if melancholy overwhelmed us. We existed in a world of unwavering piety, where anything could be surmounted through faith and prayer.

Talk of war was discouraged and talk of our families was only allowed if it did not cause us distress. The sisters told us that Mary was our Mother and God was our Father; they were always with us and always would be, so we had no cause to feel alone or abandoned.

Our days were rigorously structured. We attended chapel three times and worked, learned and prayed in between, with the exception of Sundays and Feast Days when the quantity of prayer increased. We knew what time it was and where we should be by the ringing of different bells.

There was the bell-tower bell, which rang with a dull clang, announcing prayer times and indicating that we should be in the chapel. The high-pitched, chiming refectory bell signalled mealtimes. If the nuns needed to attract our attention for anything else, they would ring a jangling hand bell and we would have to follow its sound until we found them, which was not always easy in a building which echoed so much.

Exploration of the convent was not encouraged, but few of us had any interest in probing its dank, pitch-black interior. There was no electricity. Most of the rooms were unused. Eerie winds whistled down the long corridors. Doors and windows groaned and heaved, and hinges and latches rattled and clanked. Tales of ghosts and poltergeists were rife.

The convent was home to around thirty working sisters. It also housed half a dozen very ancient nuns with faces like whiskery walnuts, who spent most of their time sitting by the fire in the refectory, either dozing or in prayer – although it could be difficult to discern which as both involved nodding and murmuring.

The unexpected presence of a group of little girls was a delight to them. They had not seen children for years. During their more alert moments they took pleasure in our company, encouraging us to sing or dance for them.

The only exception was old Sorella Brunilde, whose toothless face appeared to be folding in upon itself. It looked like a sheet of crumpled brown paper stuffed into her wimple. She would mutter and grumble about the noise and the disruption we caused, even if we were being quiet. Sometimes she would curse wildly, shaking her tiny fists and raving about sodomites. We didn't know who the sodomites were, but clearly they had wronged her in some way. When we asked one of the other sisters who they were, she told us that they were from the city of Sodom. This was only vaguely helpful as we did not know where Sodom was, although one girl said she thought it was the capital of England.

The sisters tolerated a certain amount of coarse language from old Sorella Brunilde, but profanities and blasphemy were not accepted. They would scold her. She would return a few choice words, mumble resentfully through her gums, usually about sodomites, and fall silent. The incident would appear to be forgotten within moments.

Shortly after our arrival, Sorella Brunilde was found outside in a state of confusion and partial undress and had to be apprehended by two of the younger sisters, who hitched up their voluminous skirts and chased the old nun at some speed around the garden. It was a mystery as to how Sorella Brunilde had managed to unbolt and heave open the huge front door in order to make her escape. It was also astonishing that such an elderly nun could run so fast.

I had left Pieve Santa Clara during the first winter chills, but they were nothing compared with the cold at the convent in Lodano. The ancient building was battered by winds which whipped from the north-east. The sisters said that the winds came from Russia, where it was colder than any of us could imagine. The start of the winter was wet, and once the rain subsided, icy sleet took its place. Hard blizzards of sharp snow soon followed. The nuns did not allow us to go outside, although the building was so draughty and leaky that we might as well have been in the open air.

The physical discomfort of the cold was not helped by the fact that I was constantly hungry.

Although I had never known anything other than rationing, I had come from an agricultural community blessed with orchards, vegetable gardens and chickens. Despite the war, sweet, fat grapes still dropped from the vines outside Zia Mina's kitchen. Fleshy tomatoes still ripened in the garden. The fruit trees still burst forth quantities of peaches, plums and pears. We had eggs and meat at least twice a week.

The government organised the collection and redistribution of foodstuffs, but abuse of the system was rife. Even good, honest families such as my own concealed undeclared harvests and sold and bartered their surplus. There was never any waste. Whatever could not be consumed or exchanged when in season would be preserved, pickled or salted.

Of course we had experienced shortages. My aunt had complained that due to the lack of decent sugar she had not been able to preserve all the peaches and cherries from her orchard. My parents had also grumbled about the price of meat, so beans and lentils had begun to appear in our meals in ever increasing amounts to replace it.

Despite the shortages, I had never experienced real and prolonged hunger at home. It was not the case at the convent.

The sisters kept a few stringy chickens which rarely produced any eggs. They grew what they could in the convent garden, but the short summers and rocky soil were poor for growing food and the quantity they produced was paltry. Even during peacetime they relied on bringing in provisions from outside.

The only food available was what our pooled ration cards would allow. Anything and everything which could be eaten was seized upon. Even bags of bones, stripped clean of any vestige of meat, were gratefully received and made into broth.

The scant allowance of pasta, which turned to glue when boiled, and the tiny rations of polenta were barely enough to ward off starvation. Our allocation of rationed bread was of miserable quality, often blackish-grey in colour and prone to go stale almost immediately. It was made with ground root vegetables instead of flour, or even silage, and would dissolve into a gummy, indigestible paste in our watery soups.

Although wheat flour had been in short supply at home, it could be procured. My parents had not had to resort to the rationed bread, which was not considered fit for human consumption and would be collected by a local farmer to feed his pigs. Those who donated their bread were given a salami or two in return when the pig was slaughtered.

Some girls had nightmares about bombs and campaigns of terror. I dreamed about jam and eggs. The sisters fretted that we were not adequately fed and decreased their own modest rations to child-sized portions. They must have been awfully hungry, but they never complained.

Our rations were brought to the convent every week, weather permitting. A very old man would arrive with his cart, which was pulled by a bad-tempered mule called Alfonso. Our attempts to pet Alfonso were not received kindly. He would snort, stamp his hooves and snap his teeth. He might have been better disposed if we had been able to spare a carrot for him. We tried to feed him handfuls of grass, but he spat them back at us.

Thankfully the ration man did not share the same irritable disposition as his mule. He could whistle any tune and sang songs about lost loves and mountain flowers. He liked to joke with us and would tell us that the churn on his cart was not full of milk, but of river water; then, as he eased the lid off, he would cry out, 'It's a miracle! The Good Lord has turned water into milk!'

I had looked forward to my ration of milk very much, but I had been used to sweet and creamy cow's milk. The milk which arrived at the convent came from goats and when I first tasted it all I wanted to do was to spit it out. It had an unpalatable, goaty tang and was full of hair. But as time went on and as my hunger grew, I became less fussy. I didn't even mind the goat hair which got stuck between my teeth and caught in my throat.

I was not unhappy about being at the convent because I understood that my parents had sent me there out of love, but I was frequently unhappy about being cold and hungry. The colder and hungrier I was, the unhappier I was.

There were thirty-eight evacuated girls in total, aged between five and ten. We were divided into groups and each group was allocated a nun who provided the role of a mother for us. My 'mother' was Sorella Maddalena.

Sorella Maddalena was around thirty years old, about the same age as my own mother. She had a pretty, heart-shaped face and kind brown eyes. We all liked her very much for she had a disposition which saw the good in everything. If ever melancholy or homesickness overwhelmed us, she would soothe us with an uplifting Bible story. She often spoke about her conversations with

God and encouraged us to speak to Him directly during our prayers. Sorella Maddalena said that God was always listening.

She gave us instructions on the correct way to pray. Her advice was practical and defined by clear rules about what was and was not appropriate to entreat. I could ask God for good things to happen. I could pray for my family's safety. I could pray that Pieve Santa Clara would be spared from the bombing raids. I could pray that my father would not be in too much pain to undertake his work at the cemetery. However, praying for self-serving material things was not allowed. I did bend this rule occasionally by asking for better bread and a little bit of butter, but I always made sure that I asked that we could all have it so that God would not think me selfish.

The hunger pangs could be managed during the day when the next meal, however meagre or unpalatable, was never more than five hours away, but it was a different matter at night. We were put to bed at eight o'clock and did not rise until six the following morning. The ten-hour span turned the quiet rumblings of my stomach into a deafening roar. Hunger overwhelmed my every thought.

We slept in dormitories, mostly two to a bed. I shared with a girl called Maria. She was also from Lombardy, but I had never heard of her village and she had never heard of Pieve Santa Clara.

Maria would often cry for her mother, who suffered from tuberculosis. She had been extremely ill when Maria had left, and Maria was convinced that she would never see her alive again. Often she would whimper in her sleep. I learned after a couple of nights that if I stroked her hair, she would quieten and sleep more peacefully. I was just grateful that she was not one of the bedwetters.

I cannot say that my nights at the convent were restful. Even when everybody was asleep, there was the constant buzz of breathing, sniffing, tossing and fidgeting. The hacking of catarrh-laden coughs filled the dormitory at all hours of the night. Most of us suffered from permanent colds.

It was not just the noise and the gnawing sensation in my empty belly which kept me awake. Although I was used to sleeping in the cramped confines of a blanket box, I was used to having it to myself. I longed for the comfort of dry sheets, which my mother would warm with a saucepan of embers on winter nights. My convent bed was damp and lumpy and full of flailing limbs and sharp elbows.

Most nights I would lie as still as I could, clutching my doll, and I would take myself for an imaginary walk around my home.

My starting point was always the garden gate, which I would push open, listening for the creak. It seemed no matter how often my father oiled the hinges, the gate would always creak. I would imagine my feet on the gravel, the crunching sound it made beneath my feet and the way I could feel it tingling through the soles of my shoes. I would stand in the very centre of the yard, turning through 360 degrees, looking out across the fields to the south, the horizon broken only by the spike of the belfry in the distance. Sometimes I would listen for the hourly bell.

I would look over to Rita's house, nestled beside her father's workshop, and across Zia Mina's vegetable garden. Whenever I thought of my aunt I pictured her in the garden, bent double between rows of lettuces, or fixing canes entwined with beans. My aunt could grow anything. Papá said that even if she planted a dead stick in the ground it would bear fruit.

When the weather was fine, our garden was always scattered with drying linens, hung from lines strung between the peach trees and draped over fences and bushes. I would imagine my mother calling me to help her fold sheets, or scolding Ernesto for leaving mucky hand-prints on them.

Finally I would turn towards the house, its pale walls shimmering against the sky. Beside the front door there was a small engraved plaque bearing its name, *Paradiso*. I liked to run my hands over the walls, feeling the heat absorbed from the sun and watching little lizards darting in and out of the cracks. Ernesto said that if you pulled off their tails they could grow a new one.

The part of the house in which I lived with my parents comprised only a kitchen and a bedroom. Both rooms were simple and sparsely furnished. There were two pictures on the kitchen wall: one was a charcoal sketch of Paradiso drawn by my father, and the other was a colour photograph of Pope Pius XII, sporting the red Papal mantle and a stern expression. We called our part of the house 'the annexe'.

Zia Mina lived in the main house, which was separated from the annexe by a laundry room. My father had intended to divide part of it into a bathroom for us, but his accident had quashed that ambition. The laundry room led through to Zia Mina's kitchen, where I would imagine the sweet scent of a cauldron of jam bubbling on the stove, and the smell of basil, freshly-cut parsley and nutmeg.

As I lay in the convent bed, in my mind I would climb the stairs of Paradiso and enter the bedrooms one by one: Zia Mina's room with its lace curtains and the big crucifix above the bed; Ernesto's room with his ten tin soldiers lined up on his bedside table; and the spare room with twin beds for the rare occasions when we had guests. Finally, I would find myself in the bathroom we shared. How I missed hot baths!

I tried not to think about soldiers searching our house, about bombs falling on the village or about never being able to return home. I thought about Rita and I missed her. I also thought about Ernesto, deciding that if he had not been killed, but instead had been evacuated to a convent or to a monastery, he would probably have caused chaos.

There was no doubt that I felt safe, hidden away at the Convent of the Blessed Virgin. As my mother had promised, there were no soldiers and the night was never interrupted by gunfire. The mountains were silent and empty. We had been taken to a place so remote that it was impossible to tell there was a war. I did not have any idea where I was. I just knew I was far away from everywhere.

CHAPTER 4

My first experience of school was at the convent. Education had been delayed by the start of war for many of us, so I had never been to school.

Sorella Maddalena organised the classes. We were divided into two groups, one for those who could read and one for those who could not.

I had learned my letters with my father, but I had not yet progressed to proper fluent reading. I could recognise my own name as well as the words 'apple, pear, potato' and 'cabbage' all by myself. I could also recognise the word Paradiso because it was the name of my house – but unfortunately none of these words had been useful to me for the reading test. I was therefore placed with the non-readers, something which I did not like at all.

Sorella Maddalena taught us to read phonetically, building words letter by letter. It took only a few lessons for me to master reading and I was moved to the higher class. I progressed quickly to writing, but as we did not have any slates, exercise books or paper, we would write in charcoal on the refectory wall, which would be washed down at the end of the lesson.

Within a few weeks I could write out the *Ave Maria* in Italian without any mistakes. It was not long before I could also reproduce it correctly in Latin.

Being in a convent immersed me so deeply in faith that I embarked upon a constant internal conversation with God. I spoke to Him about my worries and fears, but He did not speak back to me, as Sorella Maddalena claimed He did with her. When I questioned why this was, Sorella Maddalena told me that God spoke back in many ways. He could send signs. She told me the story of Gideon, who had asked God for a sign. Gideon had spread a fleece on the dry desert ground one night and asked God to prove He was listening by making it wet. When Gideon woke the next morning, the fleece was soaked. I attempted a similar experiment by placing my dry handkerchief under my bed one night, but when I checked the following morning it was as dry as when I had placed it there.

The sisters would wake us at six and we would file down to the chapel, which was by far the coldest part of the convent. Through the winter, the pews were permanently covered in a waxy frost and we could always see our breath. During Mass, the nuns allowed us to wear the blankets we had been given for the journey. We wrapped the scratchy brown covers around ourselves and must have resembled rows of miniature monks kneeling in prayer.

None of us looked forward to chapel very much, particularly in the morning as our first prayers were before breakfast and most of us had only slept for a few hours. The rumbling of our little bellies echoed as prayers were recited.

The rhythmic chanting of the *Salve Regina* and the response of '*Ora pro nobis*', which we repeated again and again would make our sleepy eyes even heavier.

Yawning during these prayers was severely frowned upon and any child who appeared excessively somnolent would receive a stern look from one of the nuns. Serial and habitual yawners were sanctioned with earlier bedtimes.

I became fascinated by the echo in the chapel. It could make the voice of one nun sound like three, and the small choir of sisters sound like a chorus of many. I concluded that the acoustics must make it easier for God to hear, but wondered whether He might be bored listening to the same sacraments recited repeatedly, day after day. I also wondered whether God ever yawned. I asked Him, but as usual received no answer, then felt guilty about having wasted the Holy Father's time with such a flippant question.

One afternoon we were called to congregate in the refectory. Sorella Maddalena announced that we would be forming our own children's choir. This news was met with a mixture of apprehension and excitement as the process would involve an audition.

We all knew the words to the *Ave Maria* as we had heard it recited so often, so one by one we were called to the top table to sing it as best we could. We all passed. The bar had not been set very high.

Our first few rehearsals made Sorella Maddalena wince, but after several sessions of diligent practice we became rather more melodious.

'*Brave! Brave!*' she said. 'You are singing like angels!'

The Feast of the Immaculate Conception, held on 8 December, was the most important day of the year for the sisters. Careful preparations were made and our choir was schooled and polished until we were word and note perfect. We were even allowed to miss midday prayers two days running in order to rehearse.

Sorella Maddalena flushed with pride as we sang in pious unison in the chapel. We even staged a concert for the elderly nuns later that day in the refectory. Old Sorella Brunilde screamed that we sounded like strangled cats and had to be ushered out firmly by two of the younger nuns.

But the day after the concert I awoke voiceless and with a searing pain in my throat. I tried to ask Maria to fetch one of the sisters, but no sound came from my mouth. I was moved immediately to the infirmary.

I had caught a fever. Until then I had coped remarkably well with being away from home, but the fever made me so poorly, miserable and homesick that I prayed I would die of it. Not even my dolly, who had been reduced to a sweat-soaked rag and had lost her one remaining arm, could comfort me.

Sorella Maddalena came several times each day with bread and broth, which I could barely swallow as my throat was so sore. She was my only companion as I lay quarantined, but despite her soothing words and the cooling, damp cloths with which she dabbed my forehead, I was inconsolable.

She took me from my bed, sat me on her lap, wrapped her skirts around me and cradled me, singing soft lullabies. She didn't seem to mind the slimy stream which dripped from my nose and left a long, damp smear on her scapular. I nestled against her, feeling the warm roughness of her woollen habit and the soothing cadence of her songs. The love I felt from her was deeply maternal. Although I was grateful, it made me miss my mother terribly. In a fit of pitiful weeping, I told her that I wanted my mother.

'Of course you do, my love. And she wants you. You will see her again soon enough. You just have to be brave in the meantime.'

Despite her words, bravery was something I could not muster.

'I miss my mother too,' she told me. 'It's been five years since I last saw her.'

This only made things worse. Five years was most of my life! The thought of that amount of time away from my parents was unimaginable. I shuddered deep in my heart.

'Won't you ever see her again?' I asked, my voice cracked and thin.

'Of course I will. But my family live a long way away, right up in the north, near Austria. It hasn't been possible with the war.'

'If I can't go back to my parents, will I have to become a nun, like you?'

Sorella Maddalena smiled. 'You will go back to your parents, my love. And whether you become a nun one day will be entirely your choice. Nobody is forced to take vows nowadays. It will be up to you.'

'Why did you become a nun?'

'I chose to give my life to God because I think it will be better spent serving Him, the poor and the sick, than living a secular life.'

'How did you know that's what you wanted to do?'

'That's a very clever question for such a little girl to ask,' she said. 'Giving one's life to God is a calling and an enormous commitment. It's like a marriage.'

'A marriage to God?'

'Yes.' She raised her left hand and showed me a little silver ring on her fourth finger. It was no thicker than a piece of wire. 'This ring is a symbol of my marriage to God,' she said.

'I think God must be very happy to be married to you. You're very pretty.'

Sorella Maddalena kissed the top of my head. 'God doesn't mind what any of us look like,' she said. 'We are all perfect in His eyes.'

*

I was ill for over a week, but finally my fever subsided, my throat healed and I was able to find a glimmer of my usual stoical cheeriness. However, my illness had left me weak, and overwhelmed with a craving to eat meat. Our meat rations had dwindled to almost nothing and the focus of my food fantasies had shifted from jam and preserved fruit to chicken and ham.

I prayed hard for meat. I knelt in the chapel with my hands clasped so hard that my knuckles turned white. I explained to God that I was not being selfish and asked that please, could He provide some meat – of a decent quality and not just some slimy bit of offal in soup. I wanted meat into which I could sink my teeth. I wanted meat which I could feel in my mouth and chew.

My obsession with it grew and I even wondered if it would be possible to trap some of the crows which landed in the convent garden. Zia Mina had roasted pigeons before and although I had not been particularly keen on their gamy flavour at the time, now the thought of them made my mouth water.

It was two days before Christmas when my prayers were quite miraculously answered. An old man and a young boy appeared at the convent. They were hardy, red-faced mountain people, dressed in furs and animal skins. Between them they carried the carcass of a wild boar, which was tied to a stick by its feet.

There was such jubilation at the arrival of the animal that we girls and even some of the nuns wept and we were called to the chapel to give thanks.

The boar was mounted on a spit and roasted for fifteen hours. We gathered around the fireplace in the kitchen, taking turns to rotate the spit as the animal browned and crackled. Its scent wafted through the building, cloaking the smell of damp with a mouth-wateringly meaty aroma.

On Christmas Eve we had a feast of roasted boar, bean stew and mashed potatoes. The meat was so tender that we could cut it with our spoons, and it was so succulent and flavourful that the pleasure of eating it made our heads spin. The dish was followed by a pudding made with rice and something which was almost like jam. By the end of the meal we were food-drunk.

Many of us struggled to stay awake during midnight Mass, partly because it was hours past our normal bedtime and partly because we were suffering from the effects of a hearty meal. The sisters did not seem to mind, even when they had to carry some of the younger sleeping children to their beds.

I finally had confirmation that God did listen and that He did answer prayers. I told Sorella Maddalena how I had prayed for meat.

'There,' she said. 'I told you that God always hears your prayers. But He has a lot of people to listen to. Sometimes you just have to be patient.'

*

The only communication we had from our parents during the entire stay was just after the Feast of the Epiphany. One morning the nuns informed us that a delivery would be arriving later that day containing letters and parcels from our families.

The anticipation made emotions run high and many girls began to squabble. The sisters responded swiftly with threats of confiscation of the contents of any parcel received by the perpetrators. All differences were immediately put aside.

In the late afternoon as the light was fading the ration man appeared. Rather than food parcels, however, he lifted several sacks from the back of the cart. I had been talking to God more than usual that day, praying that there would be a parcel for me. The thought of holding something which my parents had touched overwhelmed me with the desperation to be reunited with them.

When we congregated in the refectory, my heart was beating so fast that I hardly paid attention to the prayer of thanks which was being recited.

My friend Maria whispered, 'If they've sent gifts, that means our parents are alive!'

I had been thinking the same thing.

As the chorus of 'Amens' faded, I raised my head and opened my eyes. Several nuns stood by the top table, each with a sack at her feet. We were told that each sister in turn would take a parcel and call out the name of the child to whom it was addressed. That child would go and collect their package and take it back to the table. No parcel could be opened until every child had sat back down.

The allocation of parcels was a long process and one wrought with anxieties as nobody could be certain that everybody had received a package. I glanced from child to child at my table. A little girl opposite me was the first to be called. She scuttled up to the top table with such excitement that Sorella Maddalena had to tell her not to run. She came back to the table clutching a box tightly to her chest then sat down, and breathing heavily, rested her head on her precious package.

I was waiting a long time whilst those who had been called shivered with excitement and those who had not stood in dread. I prayed with all my might that there was a parcel for me, confiding to God that my desire was not the selfish wish for gifts, but the longing for something which connected me to my parents. Anything would do. I wouldn't care if all they had sent was a handful of gravel from our yard. So engrossed was I in my prayer that I did not notice when my name was called. It was only the poke of an elbow in my ribs, delivered by Maria, which roused me. Mine was the last addressed package to be handed out.

There were indeed children who had received nothing. Maria was one of them. She stared down at the table. Her hand was in her mouth. She was chewing her fingers.

'Who has not received a parcel?' asked one of the sisters. Half a dozen hands were raised. 'We have parcels which have lost their labels,' she continued. 'Some did not survive the long journey very well. Would those of you who have not received a parcel come to the front, please?'

Unlabelled packages were handed out until every girl in the refectory had something before her. The excitement fizzed like electricity. Eager fingers were poised.

Once the nuns had told us not to damage the boxes and paper and to keep the string, consent was given that we could open our parcels.

Mine contained a blue cardigan with glass buttons. It was too small for me as I had grown. It also contained more socks, an embroidered handkerchief made by my mother, four very stale fig biscuits made by my aunt and a letter from all of them written by my father. He had sketched a cat and a chicken at the bottom.

I cannot describe the exhilaration and excitement I felt at being able to read their words. They were well. They missed me. Everything at home was all right. The cat had given birth to five kittens. They had plenty of eggs.

I read the letter again and again, feeling so full of joy that I thought I would burst, but when I looked up, Maria was sitting there quietly, prodding at the contents of her parcel.

'It's not from my mother,' she said. 'She didn't send this.'

'How do you know? Maybe they didn't give you the right parcel.'

Maria shook her head. 'All of us who didn't get a parcel with a label got the same thing,' she said, pointing down the line at another grave-faced girl.

It transpired that each of the overlooked children had been given some kind of garment, plus a slightly shrivelled apple. Nobody believed that this homogenised array of gifts was from their own parents. The consensus was that their parents were dead and the nuns had concocted a lie to comfort them.

From that moment Maria became consumed with a melancholy so deep that she never wanted to play. She would sit in silence and, despite the sisters' encouragement, barely touched her meals. I tried to make her feel better by giving her one of my biscuits and my blue cardigan. She didn't eat the biscuit and just sat quietly fiddling with the glass buttons.

When it rained, the convent walls ran with brownish water and buckets were placed appropriately to catch the streams from the leaking roof. My precious letter, which I had vowed to keep forever, suffered from the pervasive damp. Within a couple of weeks, my father's words dissolved into an illegible grey blur. Eventually, all that was discernible was the shape of the cat.

Receiving communication from my parents was a mixed blessing. Although I had confirmation that they were alive and well, my every thought became consumed with the wish to be reunited with them and to be home, where everything was comfortable and familiar. It was the same for the rest of the girls.

The sisters reminded us frequently that the reason we had been entrusted into their care was that our parents loved us. They told us the story of Joseph, whose father loved him more than anyone else on earth; and the story of Abraham who loved his son Isaac so much that he was prepared to sacrifice him to God. Although this story troubled me and I struggled to understand the metaphor, I knew that the sisters cared for us deeply and the story was meant as a comfort.

I preferred the tale of Noah's Ark, which Sorella Maddalena liked to recount.

'God asked Noah to save all the animals,' she said, 'so he built an enormous ark on which they would be safe. This convent is like your ark. You are all here to be safe and out of harm's way whilst the deluge of war rages. When the war is over and the dove of peace returns you will all be taken home safely.'

The thought of God sending birds as signs intrigued me. I looked outside whenever I could, hoping to catch a glimpse of the dove which would signify that peace had returned – but apart from countless crows and sparrows, I saw only the occasional wood pigeon.

*

The winter could not last forever and thankfully as February gave way to March, the wintry winds subsided, the days lengthened and the sun began to dry out the sodden building. At last windows could be opened.

Despite the lack of adequate food, I grew. I had been aware of my sleeves becoming shorter, which did not trouble me too much, but I had also been painfully conscious of my boots becoming tighter. I had taken to wearing them without socks, which caused chilblains and blisters. Concerned by my hobbling and aware that I was not the only one who had outgrown my clothes, the sisters organised clothing exchanges.

I was allocated an itchy green skirt with a stain on the front and a burn on the hem, and a stiff brown jumper which smelled of damp.

I would have been most unhappy had it not been for the fact that I was also given a pair of shiny red leather shoes which were almost new and fitted as though they had been made for me. They were not the rustic, hard-soled boots I was used to. They were beautiful things, crafted from soft, pliant leather. I buffed them every day with my mother's handkerchief.

April burst forth with warm sunshine, and although I still could not see or hear any doves, the rattle of wood-peckers and the cooing of cuckoos in woodlands surrounding the convent filled the air. There was a newfound cheerfulness and relief that we were no longer battling the wind and the wet. Those of us who had colds were in the minority as opposed to the majority.

The sisters took us out along steep mountain paths and through the pinewoods to collect early forest fruits and to pull wild garlic from the ground. We each carried a stick, which we were told to beat on the ground before we ventured into any shrubbery or overgrowth to scare away vipers.

I did ask myself why anybody would choose to live in such a wild place, with its cold weather, its poor soil and its poisonous snakes. It didn't surprise me that so few people did live there. We trekked many miles from the convent, but we never saw a single habitation apart from an occasional tumbledown shack in which the nuns said goat-herders sheltered during summer nights.

Although I thanked God repeatedly for having sent the boar, I began to find my conversations with Him irritatingly one-sided. I could appreciate the fact that His attention had to be shared amongst many people, but I reasoned that most of us must be asking for the same thing. We all wanted the war to end so that we could go home. I questioned whether He was listening at all and how, if He was so loving and dedicated to His children on earth, He had allowed a war to happen in the first place. I began to wonder whether the arrival of the boar had simply been a fortunate coincidence.

I voiced my doubts to Sorella Maddalena, who told me to be patient, to keep my faith strong and to continue praying. Her answer did not satisfy me, but I did as she said.

That morning at Lauds as I knelt I clasped my hands tightly and concentrated with all my might on one single thought. *End the war. End the war. Please God, God please. End the war. Let me go home.* I repeated the prayer over and over, focusing on each supplication with such fervour that the words seemed to burst out of my heart. By the time I had finished, I was exhausted.

'Are you listening to me, Father?' I whispered, but there was no reply.

As we left the chapel and crossed the courtyard, I looked for signs. I desperately wanted to see a white dove, like Noah, but only swallows sliced past.

'Sorella Maddalena, what sort of bird signs does God send? Is it only doves, because I have only seen swallows,' I asked in exasperation.

'No, my dear, it's not only doves. Signs can take many forms – and perhaps those swallows *are* signs. They come here every spring. This is their home where they raise their young. Maybe they are a symbol of your return home.'

Sorella Maddalena was right. Three weeks later we received news that the war was over and we could go home.

CHAPTER 5

It was several weeks before transport could be organised to take us back home. Roads and bridges had been damaged or destroyed and fuel was in scarce supply. By the time provisions were made, I had been away almost eight months.

The scene in the piazza could not have been more different from when I had left. There was cheering, waving and jubilation as children were reunited with their mothers and in some cases even their fathers, for many men had returned from the war.

My mother and my aunt were waiting amongst the crowd in the piazza. I ran towards them faster than I had ever run. They did not recognise immediately as I was taller, thinner and my hair had grown past my waist.

They sandwiched me between them, kissing me, stroking my hair and squeezing me hard.

I showed them my beautiful red shoes and apologised for the fact that I had not been able to wear the cardigan they had sent as it had been too small. They assured me that they didn't mind at all.

'I can read now,' I said. 'And write. I read your letter all by myself!'

They clucked and fussed as we made our way home, hand-in-hand. I told them about the sisters, the other children and the choir. I did not tell them about the insufferable cold or the hunger, although it was clear to them that during my time away I had not been well nourished.

As we neared Paradiso, I saw my father. He was sitting on a kitchen chair on the verge, waiting for me. He waved and called my name and I hurtled towards him. His face was wet with tears. I was so overjoyed to see him that I clung on too hard and hurt him. During the time I had been away his general movement had improved, but he was still plagued with frequent, paralysing back spasms.

The winter had been harsh in Pieve Santa Clara, I learned. Fog had lain thick over the fields for months, and rationing had become so severe that food was sparse even for those with access to a garden. There had been weeks, it transpired, when my parents and my aunt had been forced to eat the vile ration bread.

Food on the black market had doubled, trebled and then quadrupled in price. Meat was only marginally less expensive than gold. People had taken to queuing all night to be first in line when the local shop opened, but often there was nothing at all to buy.

I heard stories of peace celebrations in towns and cities, where people had thrown parties in the streets, climbed statues and jumped into fountains, but this did not seem to apply to Pieve Santa Clara. There was relief that the war was over and a fragile sense of hope that normality would return, but nobody could be sure what form that normality would take. People were exhausted. The end of war did not mean the end of rationing and most families, including my own, had been left incomplete.

When I went to Ernesto's room I found that everything was still in its place. His clothes were folded neatly in his chest of drawers and the bed was made. His ten tin soldiers were still lined up on his bedside table. The only difference was a blur of black, sooty blooms on the ceiling, left by the smoke of the oiled rags.

Zia Mina carried on with her day-to-day chores and still tended her garden, but there was a profound sadness about her and an emptiness in her eyes. I had not been there to witness the months of her deepest despair, but I learned that she had spent countless days shut in her room, so immobilised with grief that she had barely been able to leave her bed. My mother and Ada Pozzetti had kept a vigil around my aunt in the weeks that followed Ernesto's death for they were afraid she would try to end her own life.

My delight at being reunited with Rita was immense. We hugged and skipped around one another, squealing. Rita said she had missed me so much she did not know how she had survived. She had kept my rag dolly with her the entire time I was away.

Both our dollies were battered and shabby now, but like us, they had survived the war.

Rita said that after I had left, dozens of German soldiers had swarmed into the village. They searched all the houses again and again, and were very angry that the children had been evacuated. A few days later the Allied bombings had begun with force. Although mercifully, Pieve Santa Clara was never hit, the attacks sent hundreds more German soldiers running for cover in the village.

I was a little jealous when Rita told me that throughout the incursions she and her mother had lodged with my parents and my aunt. At the time I did not understand the fear they must have felt as they cowered in the cellar night after night in the pitch black, praying that they would see the morning. My time at the convent, which had sometimes seemed so difficult, had been a holiday in comparison with Rita's experience.

I had spent my time surrounded by children, but Rita had seen nobody of her own age for many months, apart from Miracolino, a feral boy who lived by the canal. Miracolino was no playmate. He was wild and savage. Ernesto had chased him away many times when he had caught him trying to sneak into Zia Mina's garden to steal cherries or peaches from the trees.

With Ernesto gone, there was nobody on guard and during my time away Miracolino had started venturing into the garden. My aunt had caught him eating her radishes, but she had not been angry. She told him that if he was hungry, which inevitably he was, she would give him what she could.

From that day on Miracolino would often be seen standing immobile in the yard, waiting for my aunt to notice him. He seemed to function only at two speeds, either motionless or running at full pelt. He was unable to formulate sentences any longer than three or four disjointed words. He had a wild, blank stare and never closed his mouth for very long. He would roll his tongue between his lips and wipe the dripping saliva against his shoulder. Sometimes he would bite his tongue until it bled. Although she fed him, my aunt would not allow Miracolino into her house for he carried with him fleas, lice and nits. Miracolino was always scratching.

I had shooed him away, but my aunt scolded me and told me not to be hostile.

'But he's got fleas and lice, Zia Mina!' I protested. My head itched just at the thought.

'Nobody is obliging you to get close enough to catch them,' my aunt replied tersely. 'I have told him he can come and see me if he wants. That little boy needs helping. You cannot imagine the conditions in which he lives. It's not his fault he has lice, or that his clothes are dirty.'

'Why doesn't his Mamma wash his clothes?'

'Because she can barely look after herself and she is raising three children all alone.'

Miracolino's mother could be spotted from time to time wandering along the road towards the village. She was bone-thin and usually inappropriately dressed for the climate. I had seen her in summer, bundled into a coat so enormous that it seemed to be swallowing her, yet I had seen her out in the cold dressed in shirtsleeves, scratching at the scabs which covered her arms. Her speech was slurred and sometimes she would yelp or burst out laughing for no reason. Most of her teeth were missing.

She had never been married, but had managed to produce at least three children: an older girl, who never ventured far from the

61

house and would run away making a whooping noise if anyone approached her; Miracolino, and a baby which had appeared at some point during the war. There were rumours that there had been more, fathered by an unknown assortment of drunks and vagrants. Speculation and lascivious gossip abounded. My aunt said that the men who took advantage of her were feckless. I didn't know what feckless meant, but I knew it was not a desirable quality.

One day Miracolino's mother had come to Paradiso and tried to sell my mother a bag of festering rags. She cradled and bounced the tattered bundle in one arm as though it was a baby. Hooked over her other arm was an actual baby. It was a pale, limp, semi-naked little thing.

My mother had refused the rags, but given Miracolino's mother a piece of clean blanket in which to wrap her infant and sent her on her way with a jar of soup.

The name Miracolino, meaning little miracle, had come about when he was only a few months old. Nobody could be entirely sure of the name his mother had given him at birth – perhaps even she had forgotten – but the circumstances surrounding his re-naming were common knowledge in the village.

The infant Miracolino had been entrusted to his older sister. She was affectionate towards him, but she was a simple and absent-minded girl who had a compulsion to hang things from trees. She would wander up and down the path by the canal, picking up whatever she could find; thus the trees which surrounded the shack in which she lived were adorned with pieces of sacking, tin cans, bottle tops and all manner of rubbish.

Whilst Miracolino was in her care she had been distracted by something and had placed him on the ground, but the baby had rolled down the bank and into the canal.

The sister had run to their closest neighbour to raise the alarm, but the woman had been unable to understand her. Later that day, Miracolino was found almost a kilometre downstream.

A farmer had heard a strange noise coming from the water. When he had gone to investigate he found the baby boy wedged in a forked branch, blue with cold, but alive and inexplicably unscathed. It may have been his ability to remain totally still which saved his life, for if he had struggled he would most certainly have fallen back into the water and drowned. As it was, he had travelled all that way downstream and survived. Perhaps it was this experience which had taught him that in order to be safe, immobility was the best option. Whichever it was, his survival had been nothing short of miraculous and from that day everybody referred to him as Miracolino, the little miracle.

The incident had left him with a fear of water, as might be expected. This also applied to the act of washing in it, but Miracolino continued to live beside the canal which had nearly taken his life and fished its waters, always standing at a safe distance on the bank.

Zia Mina said that without the fish his family would have nothing to eat. His mother would boil whatever he caught in a little tin pot over an open fire, adding leaves to flavour the broth. My aunt gave Miracolino vegetables whenever she could. She said that fish broth and leaves was a dismal diet for a growing boy. One day she had given him two potatoes. He had eaten one raw right in front of her, biting his way through it as though it was an apple.

Miracolino had brought Zia Mina a fish as a gift to thank her for her kindness. As my aunt was not home, he left it on her kitchen windowsill, where it spent several hours maturing in the sun. Although Zia Mina was touched by his gratitude, the fish was so rank that she had picked it up with her spade. She had tried to feed it to the cat, but it had backed away in disgust.

Nevertheless, I was not comfortable with Miracolino's appearances. I did not like being stared at and I could not help but start scratching just at the sight of him.

Miracolino was not the only new face at Paradiso. Home was not the same as when I had left and it was not just Ernesto's absence which made things different.

The German troops had gone, and instead, ranks of demobbed Italians had taken their place. Pieve Santa Clara was full of dazed strangers. Weary, hollow-faced young men, still dressed in the remnants of their uniforms, gathered in clusters in the piazza, clouds of smoke from pipes and cigarettes floating above them. Some were bandaged; some hobbled on crutches; others walked with obvious injuries. Even those who appeared undamaged had an air of hopelessness and destitution about them.

Many turned up at our house. They were not local men, but men from other regions who were in transit and waiting to be transported home. Some begged for paid work, others demanded it. Most simply required a few kind words and a little charity.

Zia Mina let them sleep in her barn if they asked for lodgings and gave them vegetable broth every evening into which they dipped their bread rations. They would gather around the gate or sit around the yard slurping the thin soup from tin cups and talking about the war.

My mother forbade me from being in the yard when they congregated to eat, saying that their language and the stories they told were unsuitable. For years I believed that 'atrocity' was a swear word.

Rita's father had not yet returned, so she quizzed every new soldier who turned up or who passed along the road.

'Do you know my Papá?' she would ask. There was always desperate hope in her voice.

'What's his name?'

'Luigi Pozzetti.'

'I don't know. What does he look like?'

'He's got a moustache.'

This was the only information that Rita could give. She had not seen her father for almost four years and couldn't remember anything else about him.

Some of the soldiers would ask a few more questions. What regiment was he in? Where was he fighting? Rita didn't know. Eventually the soldiers would shrug and say, 'Sorry, no.' Rita would hang her head and wait for the next new face to come along.

The soldiers' clothing was a patchwork of miscellaneous military salvage. Much of the Italian army had been woefully equipped. American boots, English breeches and German jackets had been appropriated to replace the worn-out Italian uniforms. It did not matter whether the item came from friend or foe. Clothing was clothing.

Italian officers had benefited from good quality uniforms made from hard-wearing woollen cloth, but the soldiers who congregated in our yard were ordinary troops, a collection of disparate conscripts and formerly optimistic volunteers. Their uniforms were made of cheap mixed fabrics which were uncomfortable to wear and did not weather well.

Their jackets had only three buttons as a further form of military saving, but most had broken or been sheared off. My mother, who was a hoarder of buttons, scraps of thread and anything else useful for sewing, did what she could, sewing mismatched buttons onto their jackets so that they could do them up and not be cold. When she ran out of real buttons, she fashioned substitutes from pieces of wood, bottle tops and anything else of a vaguely appropriate size. She made thread holes by driving a nail through them. When she ran out of thread, she made her own by unpicking rags.

Word soon spread and it seemed that no soldier could pass through Pieve Santa Clara without visiting my aunt for soup and lodgings and my mother for clothing repairs.

One such man was Salvatore Scognamiglio from Naples. His right hand had been damaged during the war and he could not use it to pick anything up. He would clasp it in his left hand, massaging the fingers and straightening them out, but as soon as he released it, the fingers would curl back into a claw.

Nevertheless, Salvatore busied himself however he could at Paradiso. Whilst other soldiers lazed in the shade, killing time and waiting for their transport connections, Salvatore would rake the yard, collect and wash tin cups and pull weeds from the garden with his good hand.

Salvatore Scognamiglio seemed very foreign to me. He had a broad, leathery face, a complexion the colour of linseed oil and a head of tight corkscrew curls. His eyes were so dark they were almost black. At first I found his thick Neapolitan dialect incomprehensible. He did not refer to my aunt and my mother as Signora, but as Donna. He called me *criatura*, which meant 'child'.

Before the war, Salvatore had owned a restaurant in Naples with his brother, but it had been bombed. Subsequently his brother had been killed in Africa. He had no other family, except for some very distant cousins, but he could not be sure whether they were still alive. In any case, he said they were not good people and it was best that he kept away from them.

Initially Salvatore slept in the barn with the other soldiers, but one day he moved out and assembled a makeshift shelter by the gate to my aunt's vegetable garden.

'What are you doing?' asked my aunt.

'Guarding your tomatoes, Donna Mina,' he replied.

'The war is over, Salvatore. You don't have to be a soldier any more. And I don't believe my tomatoes are in any danger.'

'Oh but they are, Donna Mina. I heard some of the men say they would fill their haversacks with them before they left. They would leave you with nothing! You are an uncommonly kind woman and I could not bear to think of you going hungry due to their greed.'

My aunt considered this for a moment. There was a heaviness about her, as though even the most fleeting thought or simple decision exhausted her.

'Well,' she said finally, 'that's very thoughtful of you, Salvatore, but I wouldn't mind if they did take a few. It's been a good crop this year – the kind of crop I would have been delighted with a few years ago. But I don't have enough jars to keep much *conserva* and I can't really afford to light the stove to make it anyway. The tomatoes won't keep long. They should be eaten.'

'But you can dry them, Donna Mina.'

'Dry them?'

'Of course! All you need is sunshine and a little salt. That's what everybody does in the south. Have you never tasted dried tomatoes, Donna Mina?'

My aunt said that she had not. She was not familiar with any foods which were not typically Lombard and rather wary of anything she considered foreign.

'I don't know,' she said wearily.

As the summer receded, the last of the soldiers left, but Salvatore showed no inclination to go back home. Finally my aunt asked, 'Should you not be heading back to Naples now, Salvatore?'

Salvatore, who was raking the yard, shook his head.

'I have no home to go back to, Donna Mina. And no family. My brother was all the family I had. I have no hope of finding work in a restaurant now that my hand is incapacitated, so I don't know what I would do there. I was hoping that I might stay here for a while. You know I make myself as useful as possible, and I would work even harder if I knew I could stay. Surely you could do with an extra pair of hands?' He paused for a moment. 'And even if I can't offer you a *pair* of hands, I can offer you one which will do the work of two. What's more, I would be happy to give you my ration card to use as your own as long as I could be assured of a modest meal in the evening, and perhaps a little bread for breakfast.'

The decision pained my aunt. Even with the promise of a ration card the prospect of feeding an extra mouth through the forthcoming winter made her uneasy.

'I don't know, Salvatore,' she said.

'Let me prove myself to you, Donna Mina. Let me start by picking and drying those tomatoes for you. I promise you they will be so delicious you will wonder why you never considered drying them before.'

Reluctantly, my aunt conceded.

'Come, *criatura*. Come and help me. I need you to be my right hand,' said Salvatore, beckoning me over with his claw. 'First of all we need a cotton sheet and some nails. Do you think you could find those for me?'

We improvised a drying stand in the middle of the yard by stretching an old tablecloth between two posts and two chairs. Nailing the cloth to its supports was not an easy job. A one-handed man and an eight-year-old child did not make the most efficient of partnerships, but somehow we managed. Salvatore held the nails and I hammered them in. He muttered a prayer to the Madonna del Carmine before each blow of the hammer, and it seemed that She was listening because it was nothing short of a miracle that I did not strike his good hand even once.

That summer, my aunt's tomato plants had grown so vigorously that they had pulled their supporting canes clean out of the ground. Enormous orange-red fruits burst from each branch in tight clusters and some had grown so heavy that they had snapped off their stalks. Their pungent aroma filled the garden and beyond. Salvatore said you could smell them from down the road if the wind was right. He twisted a particularly large tomato from its stalk and contemplated it.

'*Pummarola,*' he said. 'That's what we call this beautiful thing in Naples.' He rolled it in his hand, polished it against his shirt and repeated: '*Pummarola.*'

We harvested seven buckets of tomatoes and set about washing and quartering them. My aunt hovered around us.

'Make sure you save some seeds,' she said.

'Don't you worry, Donna Mina. You will have more seeds than you will know what to do with.'

Once we had prepared them, we laid the tomatoes out on the sheet, flesh side up, and scattered salt over them.

'The salt draws the water out,' explained Salvatore. 'And once the water is gone, the essence of the flavour remains.'

My aunt had been worried about using so much of her salt ration, but Salvatore had assured her that most of it would be recoverable once the tomatoes were dry, and that it could be re-used. In fact, it would be the most delicious salt she had ever tasted as it would be imbued with the flavour of the tomatoes.

'How long will they take?' she wanted to know.

Salvatore looked up at the sky. 'A week or so. In Naples at the height of summer they can be done in a day or two. But it's late in the season and the sun is not so hot up here.'

The tomatoes were nursed with meticulous attention. Salvatore checked them continuously and shooed away any birds or insects. He would bring them in every night at dusk and put them back out at dawn.

Shortly after we had laid the tomatoes out, I spotted Miracolino loitering close by, his gaze fixed on them. A long thread of spit hung from his mouth. Not wishing to approach him myself, I alerted Salvatore. I hoped that Miracolino would run away as soon as Salvatore came out from the barn, but he did not. He remained immobile.

I watched as Salvatore made his way over to the boy, spoke to him and made gestures with his good hand. Moments later Miracolino was standing like a sentry by the tomatoes.

'He'll eat them,' I warned.

'He won't,' replied Salvatore. 'I've told him that if he keeps an eye on them and scares away the birds he can have some when they're ready and he can have some bread and cheese today.'

'But he doesn't understand anything.'

'Oh, but he does! Miracolino understands everything you say to him. He just doesn't know how to reply very well. He's never been spoken to much. His poor Mamma has trouble speaking herself, so it's only to be expected. Children learn from their parents, *criatura*.'

I was not convinced. I wanted to go and check that Miracolino was not eating the tomatoes, but the fear of fleas and lice made me stay away. Rita shared my wariness. We played with our dolls at a safe distance.

The tomatoes shrank and wizened day by day with Miracolino standing guard. Salvatore would often stand with him, talking and gesticulating. The boy seemed fascinated by his clawed hand and would mimic Salvatore's actions, curling his own filthy little hand into a hook shape.

It was not the only gesture which Miracolino copied. Salvatore had a habit of touching his testicles for good luck, which he insisted was an acceptable practice amongst Neapolitan men. He claimed that it not only brought good luck but also warded off evil spirits. However, it was not a practice of which my aunt approved and she scolded him very sternly for it.

'I'll thank you to leave yourself alone, Salvatore,' she said. 'And I don't want to see that lad fiddling with himself either.'

Admittedly Miracolino had adopted the habit with a little too much gusto. Whilst Salvatore would touch himself for a split second, the boy found it to be an altogether more absorbing experience. Rita and I watched in disgust as he stood by the drying table rubbing at his crotch enthusiastically.

'I think you've warded off enough evil, Miracolino,' said

Salvatore with a wink. 'It's just the birds and the flies we have to be concerned with now.' The boy winked back and did as he was told.

It was not just the prospect of food which kept Miracolino in the garden, but the fact that Salvatore would talk to him. When he was not on guard duty he ran errands and picked up the wide variety of things which Salvatore dropped. Salvatore said that quite literally, Miracolino was his right-hand boy.

It was not long before Miracolino began to make himself better understood, at least to Salvatore, using a smattering of basic words and a peculiar hotchpotch of Italian, Cremonese and Neapolitan dialects.

'What are these called?' asked Salvatore, pointing at the tomatoes.

Miracolino rolled his tongue between his lips with a look of intense concentration, then said '*P-P-Pummarola!*' in a broad Neapolitan accent.

'Bravo!' cheered Salvatore, clapping his good hand against his thigh.

Miracolino also slapped his hand against his thigh. '*P-Pummarola!*' he said again.

It was four days before Salvatore declared the tomatoes to be ready. The anticipation had become overwhelming. We gathered around the sheet. Salvatore was obviously excited.

'Donna Mina!' he called. 'Come and be the first to taste.'

My aunt came to inspect. Salvatore took a tomato, knocked the excess salt from it and presented it to her with a grand gesture.

'For Donna Mina, the lady of Paradiso,' he announced.

At first, Zia Mina was reticent. She bit into the tomato cautiously and chewed for a long time.

'What do you think?' There was tension in Salvatore's voice.

'That is incredibly delicious,' said my aunt finally.

Salvatore gave a jubilant shout and clapped his good hand

71

against his thigh again. 'Have I proved myself, Donna Mina? Will you let me stay?'

My aunt nodded. 'Of course you can, Salvatore. It would please me if you stayed. And I would have let you stay even if you hadn't dried my tomatoes.'

It is difficult to say whether we adopted Salvatore, or Salvatore adopted us. Whichever way round it was, Salvatore Scognamiglio from Naples became part of our family at Paradiso.

There was a warmth about him and an infectious, cheerful kind-heartedness. He was always helpful, busy and purposeful. He never complained about his injured hand, which was often the butt of his own jokes. There was no doubt that he was good for my aunt. Salvatore provided a welcome reprieve from her grief.

Zia Mina was concerned that people would think it improper if she were to let a young man live in her house. She did not want tongues to wag, so it was agreed that although Salvatore was welcome to eat in her kitchen, he would retain his lodgings in the barn. He had given her his ration card, as promised, and my aunt made sure that he was as well fed as was possible.

Salvatore worked hard in the garden, improvising ways around his injury by strapping and tethering tools to his arm, or looping them around his neck. He made himself a harness which he attached to the handles of the wheelbarrow and hooked over his head. He used his good hand for steering.

He loved to sing and was endowed with a rich baritone voice. His melancholic Neapolitan songs resounded across the garden. There was one song in particular which he sang over and over again. It was called 'Carmela Mia' and was about a soldier leaving his love.

'Carmé, Carmé! T'aggi a lassá, Nun c'é che ffá! Carmé, Carmé! Luntano a te. Chi 'nce pó

stá...' Carmela, Carmela! I have to leave, there is nothing I can do. Carmela, Carmela! I cannot stay far from you...

Salvatore's lodgings in my aunt's barn were basic. He had a mattress, a table and a shelf made from a vegetable crate nailed to the wall on which he kept his sparse belongings. He had lost everything when his restaurant had been bombed and his only worldly possessions were what he had carried with him when he had gone to war – a shaving brush, half a comb, a little tin for coins and a book about the lives of saints, which he read repeatedly.

He had two photographs, one of his dead brother and one of a pretty, plump girl.

'Who's that?' I asked as I looked at the picture of the girl.

Salvatore sighed. 'That's Carmela,' he said. 'She was my sweetheart.'

'Is that who you sing about?'

'Yes. It's an old song, but it's strange how the words fit. It could have been written especially for us.'

'Is Carmela dead too?'

'I hope not. I hope she's living happily in Naples and that she's found a good husband.'

'But why isn't she your sweetheart any more?'

'Ah. It's a long story. Naples is a complicated city where feuds are never forgotten. Our families had differences in the past. Hers didn't approve of me. Her parents thought she could do better. They were right and I hope she has. She's my bookmark now,' he said, kissing the photograph and slipping it between the pages of his book of saints.

Beside the crate Salvatore had made a little shrine for his dead brother. He placed ferns and flowers around the photograph and a postcard of the Madonna del Carmine. The image was creased and faded, but Salvatore said that it was prayers to the Madonna that had saved his life during the war. The postcard had been in his pocket the entire time. He said that Our Lady was very special in Naples. There was a big procession in Her honour every July. In the evening there were fireworks.

Salvatore made a sign of the cross, bowed his head and whispered words of thanks to Her every time he walked past, and out of respect, I did too.

CHAPTER 6

My father moved out of the marital bed and into a bed of his own in the corner of the kitchen. His contorted sleeping position and recurrent spasms meant that sharing a bed with my mother had become impossible. As I had outgrown the blanket box, I took over the vacant half of the double bed.

I would be tucked in at nine o'clock every night. My mother would tiptoe in somewhere around ten and before slipping in beside me she would sit on the edge of the bed, her head bowed and her hands clasped in her lap.

'What are you doing?' I asked one night.

'I am praying,' she replied. 'Go to sleep.'

Having spent so long in the convent and having had my prayers answered, I considered myself something of an authority on prayer.

'You're supposed to kneel to pray,' I whispered.

'Not necessarily.'

'Sorella Maddalena said you should kneel and cover your head.'

'That's only for when you're in church.'

'What are you praying for?'

'That is between me and Jesus.'

'Can I pray too?'

'Of course. Just close your eyes and pray until you go to sleep.'

'Do I have to sit, like you?'

'No. Just stay there.'

'Can I pray for Papá's back to get better?'

'Papá's back will never get better. But you can pray that he will bear the pain.'

'Have you prayed for him to bear the pain before?'

'I pray for that every day.'

'Do you think it's working?'

My mother looked at me sternly through the dim light, said, 'Go to sleep!' and bowed her head again.

I knew I shouldn't disturb my mother, but the words left my mouth before I could stop myself. 'Jesus raised Lazarus from the dead, didn't He?' I knew He had, because Sorella Maddalena had told us.

My mother did not answer.

'Was it God Who gave Him the power to do that? Because if He can do that, then it must be easy to make one man's back better.'

Again, my mother did not answer.

'I prayed for the end of the war and it happened,' I told her. 'I think my prayer helped.' Then as I lay still, the more I thought, the more questions filled my head.

'Can I pray that there will never be a war again? I don't want to go back to the convent.'

My mother looked up from her contemplation. 'It's not all about you,' she said.

'How about I pray for Rita's Papá to come home soon too?'

'Yes. That would be a good thing to pray for. Pray that he comes home strong and in good health. Then go to sleep!'

Rita had grown despondent. Our fruitless roadside vigils waiting for her father's return were becoming tedious. As most soldiers had been repatriated, fewer passed along the road. Some days none passed at all. And nobody stopped at Paradiso.

'Perhaps he's not going to come back,' she said mournfully.

'Your Mamma promised he would. She said she got a letter from the government.'

'Maybe they got it wrong.'

'She said he was a long way away where there aren't any trains and he would have to come home on a ship.'

'But what if he can't find his way home? What if he's lost?' Rita hung her head and seemed on the verge of tears.

'Do you want my dolly?' I asked.

'No. I want my Papá,' she replied.

I sat beside her, powerless to help and grateful that my own father had not been sent to fight.

We waited on the verge with our feet dangling in the ditch. We could see a long way up the road. The North Road, which passed between my house and Rita's, leading to Pieve Santa Clara at one end and the village of Mazzolo at the other, was perfectly straight. It had been paved directly over an ancient Roman thoroughfare.

I watched as a figure appeared on the horizon. Even from far away I could see it was a soldier. I could make out the shape of his haversack slung across his body.

'Maybe that's your Papá,' I said, trying to sound as excited as I could. Rita looked up briefly, then shook her head.

'It's not him,' she said miserably. 'I don't think he's ever going to come back.'

I couldn't think of anything else to say which might comfort her, so I just watched as the soldier approached us.

'Hello, little girls,' he said.

Rita, who would normally have begun her questioning immediately, didn't even say hello, which I knew to be very rude, so I asked instead.

'Excuse me, Signore, but do you know Luigi Pozzetti? He's my friend's Papá. We're waiting for him to come back from the war.'

The soldier rubbed his chin and thought hard. 'Maybe,' he said. 'What does he look like, this Luigi Pozzetti fellow?'

This caught Rita's attention. 'He's got a moustache!' she exclaimed.

'I see.' The soldier ran his finger along his own moustache. 'What sort of moustache?'

Rita said that she didn't know.

'Is it one like mine?' he asked.

Rita shrugged. The soldier crouched down, took her little hand and smiled.

'Here,' he said. 'Touch my moustache and tell me whether you think it's the same.'

Rita stared at the soldier in bewilderment, but tentatively did as he asked.

'What do you think, my darling little Rita?' the soldier said. 'Is my moustache as you remember it?'

It took my friend a few moments to understand. First she trembled. Then she cried. She hadn't forgotten her father at all. Suddenly everything was familiar, not just his moustache. He scooped her up into his arms and kissed and kissed and kissed her. Luigi Pozzetti was finally home.

Our fathers had been friends since earliest childhood. They were apprentices together from the age of thirteen and as grown men they had become artisans in their own right; my father as a builder and Luigi Pozzetti as a carpenter. They had worked together until Papá's accident, then Pozzetti had been called up to fight.

Rita's Papá had returned home thinner, but intact, from what he referred to as his 'enforced holiday'.

It was a happy reunion between my father and Luigi Pozzetti. I liked to think that it was due, at least in some part, to my prayers.

*

During the weeks following his return, Rita wouldn't leave her father's side. She sat at his feet, with her arms wrapped around his leg. I could not hold my father in the same way without risking a kick, as his spasms were frequent and occurred without warning. I wrapped my arms around Pozzetti's other leg instead.

One day shortly afterwards, Rita appeared in the yard in front of our house, calling my name at the top of her voice.

'Is your Papá there?' she asked. She seemed very excited.

'Yes,' I replied. 'Why?'

'Stay where you are! Don't move!' With that, she turned and flew back across the road.

A few moments later I heard the sound of a bicycle bell, the creak of the gate and the crunch of tyres on gravel.

'Ponti! Come and see!' called Pozzetti's voice.

I had never known my father and Pozzetti call each other by anything other than their surnames, the reason being that they shared the same Christian name, Luigi. As they had been inseparable as children, everybody referred to them by their surnames, Pozzetti and Ponti, to avoid confusion.

I went to help my father out of his chair.

'What does that madman want?' he said, smiling.

Luigi Pozzetti had fashioned a trailer to hook onto his bicycle. It was made from scrap wood and perambulator wheels. Attached to it was an old rope-seated dining chair, to which sturdy arms had been fixed.

'What on earth is that?' My father stared.

Pozzetti signalled to Rita, who climbed into the dining chair. Then, taking hold of the handlebars, Pozzetti hooked his leg over the saddle and set off around the yard, cycling and towing his giggling daughter behind him.

'What do you reckon?' he said, coming to a halt in front of us.

My father laughed. 'Are you going to give rides to the children in the village, is that the plan?'

'No. I'm going to give rides to *you*.'

'To me? What do you mean?'

'I can take you to the cemetery in the morning, and I can fetch you at the end of the day. It will save you over two kilometres' walk.'

My father stood scratching his chin uncertainly.

'Come on then – come and try it,' Pozzetti urged. 'I've made it an easy height for you to get on and off, and I've nailed these handles to the side. They're very sturdy. They should take your weight.'

'There's not much weight left to take,' replied my father. 'It's been said that my weight would double if I caught a dose of head-lice.'

With a little assistance from Pozzetti, and with myself and Rita holding the bicycle still, my father was able to step up into the trailer and to lower himself into the chair. He sat twisted in the seat, holding onto one arm with both hands.

'Ready?' said Pozzetti.

'Ready as I'll ever be,' replied my father.

Rita and I cheered as Pozzetti and Papá circled around the yard. Pozzetti was laughing. My father was pretending to, although I could see that really he was sucking the air in through his clenched teeth.

Zia Mina and Salvatore came to see what all the noise was about. Salvatore joined in with our cheering, but Zia Mina just stood quietly with her eyes on my father.

'It's a tragedy to see Luigi so diminished,' she said, shaking her head sadly. 'If you'd known him before his accident, you wouldn't recognise him today. Before, there was nothing he couldn't turn his hand to. Why, he restored this house for me. When I inherited the place, it was derelict.'

'Life can be cruel and unjust, Donna Mina.' Salvatore stroked his own clawed hand. 'You, more than anyone, know that.'

My aunt bit her lip and looked away.

'I'm sorry, Donna Mina,' he said quickly. 'I didn't mean to upset you.'

'It's the truth, Salvatore.'

'But I do believe that there's hope, even in the deepest misfortune.'

'You believe that?' snorted my aunt. 'It's easy for you to say. You've never had a child.' And with that, she turned and made her way back to the garden.

*

That first autumn of peace brought with it an abundant crop of grapes. They hung outside Paradiso in plump green bunches, sweetening as they absorbed the last of the warm sunshine. It was not just our grapes which flourished. Even those which had not been tended or pruned and had grown half wild were excellent.

Salvatore would inspect them every morning. He would pick one or two, rolling them between the fingers of his good hand.

'These are fine grapes, Donna Mina,' he said to my aunt. 'It would be a crime not to make them into wine.'

'I don't have any containers or bottles, Salvatore.'

'Leave it to me, Donna Mina.'

Over the following days. Salvatore visited every house and every farm within an hour's walk of Paradiso. He told us he was organising a co-operative.

'What's a co-operative?' I asked.

'It's when lots of people get together to do something which they couldn't do by themselves,' he explained. 'Your aunt has lots of grapes, but no bottles or barrels. There are other people who have bottles and barrels, but no grapes. If everybody gets together and helps each other and shares, then everybody has grapes, bottles and barrels – and so everyone can have wine.'

He patted my head and said, 'And you can help too, *criatura*. We will need to take an account of everything that people bring. How many bottles, what containers, and most importantly of all, what quantity of grapes. I will need your help writing it down.'

He held up his clawed right hand, sighed and said, 'This hand can't write any more. And my left hand writes so badly that not even I can read my own scrawl. Your aunt says you have lovely writing, so we will put that to use.'

A wooden vat, large enough for a small man to stand in and not be visible, was delivered to Paradiso the next day. It was rolled all the way down the road from an outlying farm. Over the following week, crates of empty bottles, tubs, basins and baths began to stack up in the yard. Lines of pot-bellied, wicker-covered demijohns appeared. The baker turned up with a large set of scales. I noted down every item, as instructed by Salvatore.

My mother, my aunt and Ada Pozzetti spent a week in a frenzy of activity, washing bottles and jamming them into bushes and any available gap to dry upside down.

The following Saturday morning, hordes of people arrived at first light, mostly on foot, carrying between them buckets, crates and sacks of grapes. I had never seen so many people at Paradiso.

I stood by the gate with Salvatore, recording everybody's name. Salvatore inspected their grapes and divided them into separate colours before weighing them. I wrote down the weights. The numbers made little sense to me, but Salvatore ran his finger down my neat columns of figures, muttering sums under his breath.

'When we know the weight of all the grapes combined and the number of people bringing their grapes, we will know how to divide out the wine. Each bottle of wine requires about a kilo and a half of grapes. Of course we have to allow for the weight of the skins, for evaporation.'

The process of treading the grapes was shared out between men and children. Men took it in turns to climb into the vat, with their trouser legs rolled up above their knees. More than one lost his footing on the slippery grape skins and emerged from the vat soaked in juice. Basins were also laid out in the yard for children to tread. We took our turns eagerly, delighting in the fruit bursting between our toes. Our feet were stained purple for days.

The scent of the grapes filled the yard with an intensely sweet and acid perfume, as though the past summer was exploding out of each fruit.

I like to think of that day as Pieve Santa Clara's peace celebration. People stayed long after the grapes had been pressed and brought what food and drink they had to share. Somebody played an accordion and couples danced themselves to exhaustion in our yard. Even my parents danced. My father held my mother and led her in an awkward, swaying waltz. Salvatore sang his beautiful Neapolitan songs late into the night. Everybody enjoyed 'Carmela Mia' so much that he was asked to sing it four times. Rita and I both fell asleep on her father's lap.

Over the following days, people came and went from Zia Mina's barn, where popping vats of young wine were beginning their process of fermentation. The vats bubbled and fizzed, pushing the empty grape skins to the surface. Some were collected to be used for grappa or to be mixed with sloes to make an alcoholic preserve. The rest were mixed back into the wine. Salvatore oversaw every visit.

'Don't remove all the skins,' he warned. 'Or the wine will go bad.'

The arrival of plumes of fruit flies signalled that it was time for the wine to be bottled. There was a lack of corks, so improvised systems of wooden plugs, scraps of rag and wax were used instead.

Ideally the wine should have been left to ferment for several months, but people were impatient and many drank it anyway. Being a child I had no knowledge of how it should taste. The rustic home-made system and the quality of the fruit was a lottery. I was given a small glass, diluted with water. I was intensely disappointed at how foul it was and could not understand why anybody would take something as delicious as a grape and turn it into something so disgusting.

Nevertheless, the wine-making was such a celebration that

nobody really cared about its quality. It was a symbol that the return of peace could bring back small luxuries and pleasures. Even bad wine was better than no wine.

CHAPTER 7

School started in September. Those of us who had missed our first year or two because of the war were grouped into a single classroom, where I was able to display my reading and writing skills with some pride. We did have the luxury of an exercise book each, but because these were still precious commodities, the teacher, Maestro Virgola, was extremely strict about only our best and neatest work being transcribed to paper. Most of the time we worked on slippery slate boards.

Because our names followed one another alphabetically, Rita and I were seated at adjoining desks, which was a source of great delight to us. However, we soon learned that school was not a place for enjoying oneself.

Maestro Virgola was a small man with piercing eyes and a beard shaped like an arrow. He wore spectacles, but never seemed to look through them, only over them. We were all afraid of him.

He punished pupils caught whispering, communicating in Cremonese dialect or not concentrating by rapping them hard on the head with his knuckles. Some children were made to kneel on their hands until their fingers turned blue. One boy was made to suck on a piece of soap as a punishment for swearing. It burned a blister onto his tongue.

But these punishments were lenient. Serious offences merited a thrashing, delivered with the long wooden ruler that Maestro Virgola carried at all times in class. When it was not being used as a threat, it was used to point at us. Maestro Virgola never called any of us by our names. He would simply point his ruler and address us as 'You, boy!' and 'You, girl!'

At the convent, if we had known an answer, we would put our hands up. Sorella Maddalena would choose the most eager-looking child or the one she thought most likely to answer correctly. This was not the case with Maestro Virgola. He preferred to choose the child least likely to know the answer. He seemed to take pleasure in our fear and our squirming. If the unlucky pupil did answer correctly, he would ask another question, phrasing it in the most convoluted way he could in order to create confusion. Incorrect answers were rewarded with a head-rapping, which meant that eventually all answers were rewarded with head-rapping.

Maestro Virgola's lessons took the form of a series of facts or formulae delivered with passionless repetition. The main points would be written on the blackboard, followed by a list of questions. He demanded silence. Any shuffling of feet or moving of chairs which interrupted the lesson would be punished with a sharp knock on the head.

Most of the time the only sounds we made were the scratching of our pens or chalk sticks and the occasional cough. Maestro Virgola would patrol the aisles between our desks, pacing slowly and deliberately, the metronomic tap-tap of his heels and his ruler stopping only as he looked over someone's shoulder.

On hearing the footsteps stop behind me, I knew that on no account must I stop writing, or look up from my work. Feeling his gaze on me, I would concentrate all my energy on not making any mistakes, holding my breath lest the slightest movement of air might blow a blob of ink from the nib of my pen onto my page; or dreading that the tip of my chalk would split, sending my chalk-stick shrieking uncontrollably across my slate.

Although I was disciplined regularly for errors in spelling or calculation, I was by no means the most frequent recipient of Maestro Virgola's corrections. I cannot be sure why I did not tell my parents about the punishments, but it seemed that nobody in the class did so either. There was a sullen acceptance that this was standard practice and should be tolerated. After all, we were fortunate to be at school. Most of us just did our best to be good, but by the end of each day our heads sported more knocks and bruises on the outside than they contained facts on the inside.

Maestro Virgola would say that teaching us was like trying to teach monkeys, and stupid ones at that.

We all suffered his punishments, but Miracolino was singled out more than anybody else. Maestro Virgola would demand an answer and our classmate would open his mouth, but nothing would come out. Maestro Virgola would rap him hard on the head, then wipe his hand on his handkerchief with a look of disgust.

Miracolino's ragged clothes were always caked in mud, or worse – but it was not only his clothes which smelled terrible. His diet of fish that was past its best, and leaves, caused him bursts of noxious flatulence. Maestro Virgola would point out the offensive smell to the whole class, expressing his revulsion and calling him a wretched, foul boy. Before long, he relegated Miracolino to a corner at the back of the classroom. The boy was small for his age and his eyesight was poor. He could not see the blackboard, so being at the back of the class made the difficult task of learning almost impossible.

Some children were mean to him, taunting him about his stinking clothes and foetid farts. Miracolino would simply stare at the ground, biting his tongue. I thought about what Salvatore had told me – that Miracolino understood everything that was said to him. Despite my misgivings, I felt very sorry for him.

'You mustn't be unkind,' I told his tormentors. 'He has been born into very unfortunate circumstances.' These were my aunt's words, repeated exactly.

Rita and I befriended two boys in the class, Pietro and Paolo. Our parents were not keen on the new friendship as the pair were thuggish boys who had a reputation as trouble-makers, but Rita and I were entertained by their swaggering, their cockiness and their colourful language. We would laugh as their boasting descended into physical fights.

With the start of school came catechism classes in preparation for our First Holy Communion. Our classes were given by Don Ambrogio and were so dreary that Rita and I were obliged to poke each other to stay awake. Each class was two hours long, although it felt a good deal longer. It was an ordeal for us, and clearly it was not particularly enjoyable for Don Ambrogio either.

The only reprieve was provided by Pietro and Paolo's occasional witticisms, but most of the time we sat in glazed silence as Don Ambrogio droned and pontificated. The only questions he asked were rhetorical. There were no uplifting Bible stories, just endless repetitive explanations about transubstantiation and the Eucharist.

'So, transubstantiation,' he would at long last conclude, 'is the process through which the substance of Our Lord Jesus Christ's body and blood are transformed into the substances of bread and wine. Although the bread and the wine still retain the characteristics of bread and wine, their substance has in fact been transubstantiated. And what did Jesus tell us about transubstantiation? In John Chapter Six Jesus said, "*I am the bread of life. Whoever eats my flesh and drinks my blood will remain in me and I in him.*" So, what does this mean?'

Although Don Ambrogio had not intended the question to be answered by any of us, on that particular morning, Paolo chirped, 'It means that Jesus makes a tasty snack.' And we all laughed.

Don Ambrogio leaped to his feet as though a firecracker had gone off under his chair. 'Out! *Out!* You disrespectful scoundrels!' he shouted.

After that incident, he banned both Pietro and Paolo from his classes permanently. Catechism classes became all the more uninspiring without them.

*

Shortly before Easter, Maestro Virgola announced that we would be sitting exams in Italian and mathematics so that he could assess what we had learned since the beginning of the school year; or rather, if we had learned anything at all.

This provoked a great wave of fear amongst us. Our imaginations filled with the sadistic punishments which could be inflicted upon us by the master if we failed. Most of all, we feared the wooden ruler. It didn't help that both Rita and I had missed almost three weeks of school due to an outbreak of chicken pox. Rita was so nervous that she cried when the news was announced. At this, Maestro Virgola rapped her on the head and told her to stop her whining immediately.

Pietro and Paolo were less concerned about the test, but suggested that if we were so bothered about it we should simply play truant on the day. Neither Rita nor I were brave enough to do this.

'My parents would only let me stay at home if I was ill,' said Rita.

'Mine too,' I added.

Pietro laughed. 'Then pretend you're ill,' he said. 'What's the big deal? If we all pretend to be ill, they'll just think we've caught something off each other.'

Rita and I considered the idea. It was not unusual for several children to be missing from school on the same day. Coughs, colds, stomach upsets and childhood illnesses such as mumps or measles spread quickly from child to child. Unfortunately, all four of us had already succumbed to chicken pox and we knew we could not catch it twice. Even Rita, who could normally be relied upon to catch every illness going, had been in robust health for months.

It was decided that faked headaches or stomach aches would

not pass our parents' scrutiny. We had to take some sort of decisive action which would not damage us permanently, but would produce credible symptoms. Various options were tabled.

'We could roll in stinging nettles,' suggested Paolo. 'Or we could try to catch lice from Miracolino.'

Rita and I were against both these ideas. Adults could recognise nettle stings and would see through the ruse very easily. Catching head-lice was all very well for boys, whose heads would be shaved, but for girls with long hair, such as us, it would be far worse and under no circumstances would we be willing to have our heads shaved. We would rather sit the test.

'How about rat poison?' suggested Pietro. 'If we only eat a tiny amount there would be no risk of death.' He claimed that he knew of a man who had consumed small quantities of rat poison throughout the war and successfully avoided conscription, but this suggestion was vetoed as being far too risky.

'I know,' said Paolo. 'Let's jump in the canal and walk around in our wet clothes until we catch a chill.'

'Not me,' said Rita. 'It would go straight to my chest and then I really would be ill.'

Finally it was my own idea which was voted the most workable. My aunt had preserved some sloes with the surplus grape skins from the wine-making, but they had gone rancid. The jar had been sitting forgotten and festering in my aunt's barn for some time. I suggested that we should eat those. We all knew that eating rotten fruit was a sure way of upsetting our stomachs and giving us the runs, and as far as we knew, nobody had ever died of that.

The day before the test I took the jar and smuggled it to school, where I hid it behind one of the lavatories until the end of the day. After school we congregated in the garden beside the church.

The rotting sloes stank. The fruit had turned into a slack, lumpy paste over which a film of fuzzy mould had grown.

Pietro, Paolo, Rita and I stood in a circle, hidden from view by a laurel bush, passing the jar between us and spooning the putrid gloop into our mouths. The acid paste fizzed on our tongues and made us retch as we swallowed it.

Miracolino had followed us. He stood staring at us and scratching.

'Go away!' said Pietro.

Miracolino did not react.

'This is none of your business. Clear off – and keep your beastly fleas to yourself,' Pietro repeated, pulling an ugly face.

Still Miracolino did not respond. He seemed to be staring right through us.

'Don't you understand Italian? Go away, idiot,' Paolo sneered in Cremonese dialect, 'or I'll throw you in the canal and you can drown, like you should have done the first time!'

Although I did not want Miracolino to join in, I didn't like the boys' meanness.

'Don't say that,' I said.

'Why not? He's an idiot. I don't even know why he comes to school.'

Pietro pulled another leering face at Miracolino, who just continued to stare.

'We could let him have a bit,' I said at last. The sloes were so foul that I knew we would not finish them.

Pietro looked at Paolo. They both looked at Rita, who shrugged, then said, 'All right. But don't tell him what we're doing.'

'He wouldn't be able to tell anyone anyway,' said Paolo. 'He's too stupid.'

I held the jar up and beckoned Miracolino over. There was a momentary spark in his blank stare.

'I'm not using the spoon after he's used it,' said Pietro, recoiling. 'I might catch idiotitis.'

'I've had enough anyway,' said Paolo, letting out an enormous, vile-smelling belch. 'And I think it's working already.'

We had managed to consume half the jar between us. I tried to take one last spoonful, but my stomach knotted and I feared that if I ate any more I would be sick on the spot. We all agreed that the dose was probably sufficient.

Miracolino edged towards us and held out his hands.

'Don't tell,' I said, passing the jar over.

'Yes. Keep your stupid trap shut, you imbecile,' added Paolo, raising a clenched fist towards Miracolino, 'or I'll make sure you have even less teeth than your mother.'

Miracolino took the jar and bolted several spoonfuls very eagerly. He didn't seem to find it unpalatable at all. He then dropped the spoon and scooped out all he could with his hands, stuffing it into his mouth and gulping so quickly it made him pant. Once he had finished he handed me back the jar and resumed his immobile, staring position.

It was not long before I was overcome with a contented warmth and strange sense of excitement, as though something particularly good was about to happen. Everything seemed funny. Even Pietro and Paolo's belching contest made me laugh. Rita tried to join in, but she couldn't belch. Instead she pulled faces which I found so hilarious that I laughed until I had tears in my eyes.

The boys entered into a heated argument about something and started to fight, which involved much shoving and toe-stamping, but their altercation was short-lived as they fell to the ground, flopping like fish and giggling.

We milled around the garden for a while until the boys suggested we should go into the church.

'Let's see if the old witch is there,' they said. 'If she is, let's creep up on her and scare her. You should hear the noise she makes when you startle her.'

The old witch they were referring to was Immacolata Ogli, the elderly parish housekeeper. Everybody in the village knew her. She had raised thirteen children – five of her own and eight fostered, one of whom had been Zia Mina, who had been orphaned as a baby. Zia Mina called her 'Mamma Imma'.

Immacolata came to Paradiso regularly to see Zia Mina, in particular during the spring and summer when she would be given some fruit, vegetables and flowers. Zia Mina grew a strip of dahlias and gladioli especially for the church, which Immacolata would collect on a weekly basis.

Standing talking in the garden, they made an odd pairing. My aunt measured over six feet in height, which was nearly a foot taller than average for a woman, while Immacolata was short, around the height of a twelve-year-old child. However, what Immacolata lacked in height she made up for in girth, and in spirit.

She was always red-faced. It looked as though she scoured her cheeks with a scrubbing brush. Her hair was a frowzy mass of grey wire which she tried to tame, unsuccessfully, with a multitude of clips and pins – except in church, where she covered it with a hat that resembled a cauliflower.

Immacolata was extremely pious and would cross herself repeatedly as she spoke, like a form of punctuation between her sentences. Despite her advanced years – and through choice, not necessity – she still worked every day, cleaning, preparing meals for Don Ambrogio and arranging flowers in the church. Pietro and Paolo said she had chased them out of the church many times before.

Rita and I followed the boys, holding hands and singing. Immacolata was not in the church. It was completely empty. It had never interested me much before, but suddenly it felt like a place worthy of exploration. We played tag between the pews, ran up and down the aisle, around the altar and ventured into the sacristy, where Don Ambrogio's robes hung on a rail. I had never been into the sacristy before, for it was out of bounds to all but the priests and altar boys.

Pietro took one of Don Ambrogio's stoles, wrapped it jauntily round his neck and promenaded around the sacristy, swinging his hips and pouting.

'Look at me,' he gushed. 'I'm such a beautiful lady.'

Rita and I laughed and laughed. For the first time in my life I felt the thrill of naughtiness. I felt brave and mischievous.

A game of hide and seek ensued. The church was so rich in exciting hiding places that each seeking took a long time. When it was finally my turn to hide I headed for the confessional, where I stayed for a long time waiting to be discovered, crouching under the priest's bench.

I cannot say how long I was in the confessional. I may even have dropped off to sleep briefly. It was only boredom and cramp which made me emerge, and when I did so I found that nobody was looking for me.

Rita was sitting on the altar steps groaning quietly, rocking back and forth with her head on her knees. Paolo and Pietro were behind the altar, attempting to break into the tabernacle.

'What are you doing?' I asked.

'This is where the wine's kept,' Pietro replied.

'Stop it!' I said. Suddenly being in the church did not seem like such good fun. My feeling of bravery had dissolved.

'Stop it!' I said again. 'You'll get us into trouble.'

Pietro came towards me, his lip curled. He was still wearing Don Ambrogio's stole.

'We'll do what we want,' he snarled, giving me a shove which sent me toppling backwards. As I fell, there was a loud clattering noise and the smash of something heavy breaking. I had tripped over an enormous Paschal candle and in so doing had knocked over the statue of a saint, which now lay maimed and decapitated on the floor.

'I'm going to tell,' I said, but Pietro grabbed my arm.

'Really? Tell what – that you broke a statue? If you try to make out we were here, we'll deny it, and we'll tell them all about your plot to miss the test.'

'It was your idea too!' I retorted, feeling anger and indignation rise through me.

Pietro brought his face close to mine. Our noses almost touched.

'You provided the poison. The sloes were your idea,' he hissed. 'And you got them from your aunt – and everybody knows about her and poison! If you tell, we'll tell too, and it's not just you who'll be in trouble. They'll come and take your aunt away and probably your parents too for protecting her.'

'I don't know what you're talking about,' I said, but Pietro just smirked.

'Oh yes, you do,' he sneered. 'Your aunt poisoned all those German soldiers! My mother said she put the whole village in danger by doing that: we were lucky we weren't all rounded up and shot. If you breathe a single word, you're going to be in more trouble than you could ever imagine. Your aunt's a murderer. It's about time she paid for what she did.'

He pulled an ugly face and drew his finger slowly across his neck.

'Your precious Aunt Zia is a murderer,' he said again.

I stood paralysed. The only thing I could think to say was, 'The soldiers didn't come to my house.'

'And we weren't in the church. Come on, Paolo. Let's go!'

Paolo leered at me and asked, 'Were you hiding in the confessional just now?'

I nodded.

'Was it a good place to take a piss?'

'What?'

He shoved past me, opened the confessional door and relieved himself copiously inside. Pietro roared with laughter and the boys began to sing in unison.

'Graziella took a piss in the confessional! Graziella took a piss in the confessional! Graziella took a piss in the confessional!'

'I didn't!' I cried.

With that, they ran out of the church, still chanting, 'Graziella took a piss in the confessional!'

'Oh no!' wailed Rita. 'We're in so much trouble.'

My head reeled with Pietro's words. Had my aunt really poisoned the soldiers? I tried to think back to overheard fragments of conversation between my parents; to my father's instruction never to say that the soldiers had come to our house; to my aunt's bottles being smashed and buried... but my brain was fogged with panic.

'We have to tell our parents,' whimpered Rita.

'No!'

'We'll be in even more trouble if we lie.'

'We just have to tidy up and if anyone says anything, I'll take all the blame. I'll say it was me who did it,' I offered.

'That's ridiculous – you don't have to do that. We should tell them what Pietro and Paolo did.'

That was when I realised that Rita had not heard my aunt mentioned.

'No,' I said hastily. 'We have to say that it was me. You don't have to get into any trouble. If you want, I can say that you weren't here either.'

'Why? Why wouldn't we tell the truth? It wasn't even your fault the statue fell over. You were pushed, Graziella. Why do you want to get yourself in all that trouble?'

'I can't tell you why, but you have to trust me. It's really important and it's really serious. If I could tell you, I would, but I can't.'

'But I thought I was your best friend.'

'You are. And you will always be. Forever. But please, just say it was all me. Promise.'

'All right,' said Rita, obviously puzzled.

The plan seemed watertight. I didn't care what punishment I would receive as long as my aunt's terrible crime did not come to light.

I pushed the tabernacle door closed as best I could. The latch was loose, but I hoped it would go unnoticed. Then I gathered up the pieces of the statue and hid them behind a column and mopped up the confessional with a prayer cushion.

Suddenly Rita said, 'What's that smell?'

'It's pee.'

'No, not that.'

'Incense?'

'No, not that either. There's a terrible smell.'

I stopped, took a deep breath and heaved. The smell was so foul that it sent a cold chill right through me. I clamped my hand to my face, covering my nose and mouth. Rita covered her own nose and mouth with her sleeve.

Miracolino was standing at the foot of the altar steps, staring at us. The origin of the repulsive smell was immediately clear.

'You shouldn't have given him sloes,' gasped Rita. 'That's the worst fart ever! How can anyone fart like that?'

She suddenly grasped her stomach. 'I need some air,' she said feebly.

We made our way back outside. I wanted to tell Rita that we should go home, but couldn't form the words. My tongue felt swollen in my mouth. I attempted to head out of the garden, but the paths and bushes rolled around me. I tried to stand still, but couldn't. The ground beneath me swayed.

Rita cried, convinced she was about to die, and was promptly sick all over her clothes. A moment later, I did the same.

All I could do was to lie down and close my eyes. For a moment

I thought I was back in the confessional. My memory flashed back to the game of hide and seek, but I could not tell what was real or imagined. Soldiers shone lights in my face. Panic-stricken thoughts about the damage in the church swirled around my head. I envisioned my aunt being led away to prison in chains.

Although he had consumed a far greater quantity of sloes than any of us, the effect had not been the same for Miracolino. He had remained inexplicably clear-headed and had run back to Paradiso to alert my parents that all was not well. They in turn had alerted Rita's parents.

Pozzetti came down to the village on his bicycle and found us slumped together under the laurel bush, semi-conscious and soaked in purple vomit. Once he had ascertained that we were not in any mortal danger, he loaded us into his trailer and took us home. Pietro and Paolo were nowhere to be seen.

Our mothers made us strip out of our vomit-soaked clothes on the front step and sponged us down, by which time we had sobered up somewhat. My parents were not angry, just utterly perplexed.

'Sloes?' said my father. 'Why on earth would you want to eat sloes?'

'Couldn't you tell that they were off?' asked my mother. 'Mina said they were mouldy! They must have been disgusting. Why would you eat something which was so obviously rotten?'

I didn't tell them about the plan to miss the test, about the incidents in the church, or what I had learned about my aunt. I hoped desperately that Rita had remembered the promise I had made her keep.

'You could have made yourselves very ill,' said my father. 'It was a silly thing to do.'

'You *have* made yourselves very ill!' my mother said, then added, 'It's just as well Miracolino had the good sense to come and tell us.'

My night was filled with panic-stricken visions of dead soldiers and of my aunt being harangued by angry villagers. At one point I thought I heard gunfire in the distance. I gripped my sheets and listened again, but it was just my father snoring. His words swirled around my head.

'If anyone asks you, even if it's someone you know, don't tell them the soldiers were here.'

CHAPTER 8

The following morning I awoke with a thunderous headache and a mouth so dry that my lips were stuck to my teeth.

I had hoped that my mother would take pity on me and let me stay at home, but she said there was absolutely no reason why I should not go to school. Rita's mother had reached the same conclusion. We trudged our way there slowly, our heads groggy and throbbing. Pietro and Paolo were absent.

We sat in silence, waiting for our test, but first it appeared that Maestro Virgola had an announcement to make. He stood at the front of the class, glowering. His scowl rested upon each of us in turn. Finally he said, 'This morning I received word that several heinous acts of vandalism were perpetrated in the church yesterday. I have agreed with Don Ambrogio that if I suspect that any one of you was in any way responsible, I would ensure that the guilty party, or parties, would receive a suitable punishment.'

He scanned across the faces in the class again. I looked down at my desk.

'Does anyone have anything they wish to say?'

I felt Rita's eyes glance my way, but I kept my gaze fixed on my desk.

'Well?' growled Maestro Virgola. 'Does anyone have anything they wish to say?'

The class maintained an innocent silence since, apart from Rita and myself, they knew nothing. Maestro Virgola snorted and began to write a list of questions on the blackboard.

'You may commence,' he said.

We sat our tests in silence as he patrolled between our desks, tapping his long wooden ruler on the floor in time with his footsteps. The exam was incredibly hard and it was not made any easier by the fact that my head was pounding. Every tap of Maestro Virgola's ruler rattled through my skull.

Rita and I decided to skip our catechism class that afternoon as we could not face the two hours of tedium we knew it would involve. What's more, questions might be asked about the events in the church. Lying to a teacher was bad enough, but lying to a priest was an altogether different matter.

I hurried home and did my best to keep out of everybody's way. I was in the garden hanging out laundry when my father and Luigi Pozzetti arrived. My father was not alone in the trailer. Cradled in his arm was the broken statue from the church.

'What have you got there, Don Luigi?' Salvatore asked as my Papá dismounted even more awkwardly than usual, trying not to drop the pieces of statue.

'It's dear old Saint Egidio. He needs a bit of medical attention.'

'Saint Egidio? Isn't he the patron saint of the physically incapacitated?'

My father nodded. 'Indeed he is,' he said.

Salvatore picked up Saint Egidio's severed hand, then looked at his own clawed hand and said, 'God has a strange sense of humour.'

*

The schoolyard was always a noisy place, but the next day as Rita and I walked in, a hush descended. Everybody stared and whispered. Gradually they began to chant Pietro and Paolo's words.

'Graziella took a piss in the confessional! Graziella took a piss in the confessional! Graziella took a piss in the confessional!'

Rita was incensed. 'Tell the truth – say who did it!' she urged me.

'No,' I replied.

Pietro and Paolo stood snickering by the gate. When I looked at them, they drew their fingers across their necks.

'Murderer!' mouthed Pietro.

As I unpacked my satchel ready for class I could feel my classmates' smirking glances. Maestro Virgola's voice barked across the room.

'You, girl. Come here!' he snapped.

A cold sweat prickled across my face as I made my way to the front of the class. I was so afraid of Maestro Virgola that I thought my legs would give way.

'Yesterday I asked very clearly whether anybody in this class had anything to say about the acts of sacrilege perpetrated in the church. Do you recall that?'

I nodded.

'Speak up, girl! Do you recall what I said yesterday?'

'Yes, Maestro.'

'And you said nothing – at least, not to me. But it now appears that you have been bragging about your odious behaviour to your classmates and encouraging them to sing about your despicable actions. So, what do you have to say for yourself today, girl?'

I hung my head and confessed to the things I had not done. A wave of muffled tittering spread through the class as I came to the part about peeing in the confessional.

'There will be punishment!' bellowed Maestro Virgola, with such force that I felt the heat of his breath as he circled around me. My whole body trembled.

It was then that Miracolino raised his hand.

'What is it, boy?' snarled Maestro Virgola.

Miracolino opened his mouth, but it took him a long time to find his words. Before he could get a single one out, Maestro Virgola yelled, '*Well?* If you have something to say, boy, say it!'

Miracolino rose to his feet and screwed up his face in

concentration, but the only sound that emerged was a stuttering grunting noise as he pointed towards Pietro and Paolo.

'What are you doing, stupid boy? Say what you have to say and stop pointing your filthy hands around my classroom! And sit down!'

Miracolino stamped his feet in frustration and continued to point at Pietro and Paolo, but he could not speak.

'Sit down, I said!' shouted the teacher again, lunging towards him with his ruler raised. Miracolino cowered and did as he was told.

'As for you, girl,' he said, narrowing his eyes as he spoke, 'I will deal with you properly later. For now, go to the back of the class. For the foreseeable future you will be doing without the comfort of a chair.'

Pietro and Paolo grinned while I was made to kneel at a desk beside Miracolino's.

'Don't tell,' I whispered under my breath.

Within a short time my knees were numb and my feet had gone to sleep. When the class was dismissed at break-time I was not allowed to go outside. I remained kneeling at my desk, attempting to copy out the lesson. From my new position at the back of the classroom I had not been able to see the blackboard at all.

The morning was interminable. As I took my satchel and prepared to leave, Maestro Virgola challenged me: 'Where do you think you're going?'

'Home, Maestro.'

'Home? I think not! Collect your things and come with me. Quickly!'

'Where are we going?'

'To see Don Ambrogio, of course. You must face him and pay for your actions.'

Rita was waiting for me in the schoolyard.

'What are you doing loitering there, girl?' barked Maestro Virgola.

'I'm waiting for Graziella, Maestro,' replied Rita meekly.

'Are you unable to find your way home without assistance? Go! Go home!'

Rita stared at me, wide-eyed and frightened. I hung my head. The door to Don Ambrogio's residence was opened by Immacolata.

'We are here to see Don Ambrogio,' announced Maestro Virgola. He moved to step inside, but Immacolata blocked the doorway.

'He's having his lunch,' she said curtly. 'You'll have to come back later.'

'This is a very important matter, Signora Ogli.'

'So is Don Ambrogio's lunch. I haven't spent half the morning cooking it for it to be eaten cold.'

Maestro Virgola puffed out his chest, but Immacolata did not seem in any way intimidated. She stood her ground with her stout arms crossed.

'Signora Ogli, it is absolutely imperative that I see Don Ambrogio immediately. It is of the utmost importance.'

Immacolata made a huffing noise and puffed out her fat cheeks.

'It better be,' she said, 'but it's very inconvenient. Come with me.'

We were shown to a dining room, where a long refectory table was set for one. Don Ambrogio was seated at one end. He was halfway through a plate of chicken with fried potatoes. A large pasta bowl sat wiped clean beside it. Immacolata took the empty bowl and waddled out of the room grumbling loudly about spoiled food.

'I have found the culprit,' Maestro Virgola boasted. 'This girl has admitted everything. It seems she has also bragged about her disgraceful behaviour to her classmates as they are all talking about it. In fact, they have all been singing about it!'

The priest wiped the grease from the corners of his mouth with the large linen napkin which was tucked into his collar.

'I have to admit, it was not you I expected to see, Graziella,' he said. 'Come in. Let me hear what you have to say for yourself.'

'I am terribly sorry about all the damage I did in the church.'

'Indeed. I struggle to understand why you would do such a thing.'

I didn't have an answer. All I could do was to apologise repeatedly and offer to make amends. Don Ambrogio clasped his doughy hands together and thought for a moment, then said, 'Is there something you're not telling me?'

'No, Don Ambrogio.'

'Was anybody else with you?'

'No, Don Ambrogio.'

'You're absolutely sure about that?'

'Yes, Don Ambrogio. I was all alone in the church. Rita Pozzetti was outside in the church garden the whole time and there was nobody else. Please don't punish Rita. She has nothing to do with it.'

Don Ambrogio took a toothpick from the table and poked at his teeth. 'Nobody else at all? You're certain about that?'

'Yes, Don Ambrogio.'

We were interrupted by a knock at the door. Rita had not gone home, as instructed by Maestro Virgola. She had run to the cemetery to fetch my father, who came into Don Ambrogio's dining room looking very concerned.

'I assume you've heard about the filthy acts of vandalism in the church?' said Maestro Virgola, looking at my father with disdain. 'Your daughter has admitted all responsibility.'

My father was shocked. He took off his hat and stood twisting it in his hands.

'Graziella?' he said. 'Really?'

I nodded.

'Why did you not tell us?'

I had managed to keep my composure until that point, but my father's embarrassment and disappointment made my lips tremble and I began to cry. He reached out his hand towards me, but Maestro Virgola interposed himself between us.

'It seems my daughter was not herself,' began my father. 'She ate some fermented sloes without realising that they were alcoholic. Of course, as she is only a small girl the effects of even a tiny amount were quite severe.'

'Are you trying to justify your daughter's behaviour by claiming she was *drunk*?' interjected Maestro Virgola.

'Well, of course I am not excusing what she *says* she did, but I feel I should point out that if she did indeed do it, there is an explanation for her behaviour, which is extremely out of character.'

'A poor excuse!' the man spat.

'A childish mistake,' corrected my father.

'And not one which can go unpunished!'

Don Ambrogio raised his hand to stop the argument and looked at me intently.

'I think that in this instance, we should be slow to chide,' he said thoughtfully. 'Perhaps you would like to consider everything you have told me, Graziella. And when you have given it some consideration, I would like you to come back and speak to me again.'

'But she has admitted everything!' exclaimed Maestro Virgola. 'What else is there to consider? This girl's actions have been appalling. An outrage not only to you, Don Ambrogio, but to the church and to the whole community – and an unimaginable embarrassment to her family!'

The priest was quiet for a moment, then turned to me. 'Are you familiar with the Ninth Commandment?' he asked.

'No, Don Ambrogio.'

'It states that "Thou shalt not bear false witness". Do you know what that means?'

'No, Don Ambrogio.'

'Well, it means that you should not tell a lie about something that has happened in order to protect yourself, or others. God instructs us all to tell the truth. I want you to think about that carefully, and when you have, come back and see me.'

I left the priest's house with my father. He had wrung his hat so tightly in his hands that it no longer sat straight on his head. He seemed at a loss for words and took several long swigs of medicine from his bottle as we walked home. I didn't tell him that I had been on my knees all morning and he didn't seem to notice that I was walking with a limp. We shuffled our way down the road together in silence.

My mother's reaction was not as calm as my father's had been.

'What?' she exclaimed. 'You did *what?*'

I repeated the list of sins, which now flowed from me with a well-practised fluency.

'Were those boys anything to do with all this?' demanded my mother.

'No,' I replied. 'And nor was Rita. It was just me.'

There was no doubt that my mother was angry, but like my father and Don Ambrogio she could not quite believe that I would do such a thing, even in a state of inebriation. My parents gave me numerous chances to amend my story, but I stuck to it. They said that as a punishment I would be given extra chores, which was exactly what I had expected. I thanked them, perhaps rather too enthusiastically.

Of course, telling my parents the truth would have been the sensible thing to do, but by this time I was in too deep. A few extra chores and a couple of days on my knees was a small price to pay for my aunt's protection. What was more, I had made Rita lie for me and I did not want to get her into trouble.

Salvatore tried to keep a straight face, but could not control his mirth.

'My brother and I stole a donkey once after a few too many glasses of Nocino,' he chuckled. 'And one man I knew woke up in the Piazza del Plebiscito stark naked apart from a saucepan on his head. But peeing in the confessional? That's quite a caper!'

I did not see the funny side.

It was the pain in my knees which woke me the following morning. Bruising was starting to bloom across my kneecaps, which were swollen and tender to touch. The thought of a second day kneeling filled me with dread. I took the old tablecloth on which Salvatore had dried the tomatoes and tore it into strips, which I bound around my knees. My improvised bandages made walking difficult and they were still slightly imbued with the smell of the tomatoes, but the binding dulled the pain and would provide padding for my second day of kneeling.

The second day on my knees was far from comfortable, but it was bearable. Miracolino kept frowning at me and I prayed that he had not eaten too much bad fish, for I was certain that the slightest whiff of fart would make me vomit.

Pietro and Paolo continued to taunt me, drawing their fingers across their necks.

'How's your aunt?' they said. 'Has she invited anyone over for a couple of drinks recently?'

I did my best to ignore them, but their goading was relentless.

I shifted my weight from knee to knee and tried to sit back on my haunches, but the pain spread down my shins and up my back. Maestro Virgola told me repeatedly to stop fidgeting.

'Stand up!' he ordered.

My knees creaked as I heaved myself upright. My legs felt as though they would not carry my weight and my feet were so numb I could not feel the floor. Had it not been for the support of the bandages I believe my legs would have buckled.

'Lift your skirt,' he commanded.

I raised the hem of my skirt by a few centimetres and revealed my makeshift bandages.

'What's this?' he demanded.

'Bandages, Maestro,' I replied quietly.

'Bandages?' he bellowed. 'Bandages? Lift your skirt higher!'

The long wooden ruler appeared from nowhere. I did not feel the pain of the first strike, or the second, or the third. All I heard was a swooshing as it cut through the air and a cracking as it hit the back of my bare thigh. I was aware of a rushing in my ears and a prickling up my spine. For a moment it felt as though I had eaten sloes again.

When I came round, Maestro Virgola was standing above me telling me to wake up. It took me a few moments to realise that I had fainted, and it was then that the searing pain branded itself into my leg. Total silence had descended on the class.

'Get up, girl! Go and wash your face. Be quick!' he said. 'The rest of you, get on with your work.'

Everybody did as they were told, except Miracolino, who ran out of the classroom so fast that several exercise books were blown off desks. Maestro Virgola bellowed at him to come back, but Miracolino was out of the building before he could finish his sentence.

I hobbled to the washroom, still dazed. My vision was flecked with spots of light and I could feel a throbbing, egg-shaped lump growing on the side of my head where I had hit the desk as I had fallen. The welts on my thighs were the colour of red wine. Trickles of blood snaked their way down my legs.

The terror I felt at the thought of going back into class was so overwhelming that despite the pain and my giddy vision, I hastened out of school. I knew I would be in more trouble for absconding, but all I wanted to do was to go home.

I only made it as far as the little garden beside the church before feeling faint again. I cowered by the same laurel bush where I had fallen asleep with Rita two days previously and cried. The empty sloe jar was still there.

I would have hidden if I had heard Immacolata in time, but my sobbing must have drowned out her footsteps. She appeared quite suddenly, barely two paces from me.

'Is that you Graziella? Why are you crying?' she asked.

I could not speak.

'Oh my Good Lord!' she exclaimed, crossing herself. 'You've banged your head. Did you fall, dear child?'

It was then that Immacolata saw my bandaged knees and the wounds from the ruler and made another sign of the cross. She bent down as far as her stout frame would allow, reached out her hand and helped me to my feet.

'Come along now,' she said gently. 'Let's get you inside and sort you out and we'll find a nice piece of cake for you to eat.'

Immacolata walked me back to Don Ambrogio's residence, murmuring words of comfort and supporting me with her arm. She had remarkable strength for a woman of such advanced years.

She took me to the kitchen and applied cold compresses to the bump on my head, tutting and muttering the entire time. The cold compresses made me flinch.

'There, there,' she clucked. 'I know it's not very comfortable, but the cold's good for bumps and bruises. Now, let's have a look at them legs of yours.'

She began to unwrap the strips of torn tablecloth from around my knees. Her old hands were a patchwork of stove-burn scars and liver spots, but her fingers were nimble.

'Been praying, have you?' she asked as the last of my bandages fell away. 'Looks like you've gone on a pilgrimage all the way to Lourdes and back on these knees.'

She inspected my legs carefully and puffed out her red cheeks.

'This weren't no fall, was it?' she said at last. 'I need you to tell me exactly what's happened. Who did this to you, dear child?'

Somehow through my sobbing she managed to understand that my injuries had been caused by Maestro Virgola.

'Does he hit all the children?' she asked.

I nodded. 'But not always with the ruler.'

'So why did he punish you so much more harshly than the others?'

'Because I was very, very naughty,' I wept.

'Very naughty? What could you possibly have done to deserve this?'

I told her about wanting to miss the test, about the sloes, about the tabernacle and the statue, but when I told her I had peed in the confessional, she said, 'No, you didn't.'

Immacolata looked at me gravely as she took a fresh bandage and began to wind it around my wounded thigh.

'Don't you tell me no fibs,' she warned. 'I'm an old woman who can smell a fib a mile off and this one fairly stinks. At a push I might believe that you broke Saint Egidio,' she said, making a sign of the cross as she said his name. 'I might also believe that you broke the latch on the tabernacle. Perhaps. But I can say with absolute certainty that you did not pee in the confessional. You see, I was the one what discovered it. I went to change the flowers in the church and I could smell it as soon as I walked past. I thought a cat had got in. But when I had a look, I knew it wasn't no cat as surely as I know it wasn't you. Do you know how I know that?'

I shook my head and looked down at my feet.

'I'll tell you how. Whoever peed in the confessional aimed at the wall when they did it. Right up as far as they could. It stripped the varnish clean off! But being a little girl, you are not equipped to pee up walls.'

Everything was just getting worse.

'So who was it that did it then? I know you know. And you need to tell me,' she said, giving a long sniff. It made me wonder whether she really could smell lies.

Finally I admitted Pietro and Paolo's involvement, although I stopped short of mentioning my aunt.

'I knew it! Them boys is nothing but trouble. And they're bullies – and if there's one thing makes my blood boil it's a bully,' she said, crossing herself again.

I had told the truth, but not the whole truth because the whole truth could never be told. However, it seemed to be enough for Immacolata. I hoped with all my heart it would be.

Immacolata gave me a generous wedge of the richest cake I had ever tasted and finished binding my wounds. She had used such enormous lengths of bandage that I could not bend my legs at all. Despite the fact that only my knees and thighs were injured, she had bound both my legs from ankle to hip. They stuck out in front of me as stiff as posts. She also bound my head. I must have looked as though I had been partially mummified.

'Well, I can promise you that you won't be in no trouble, but I do need you to tell me something else. When you came here yesterday with that beast of a teacher, what did Don Ambrogio say to you?'

'To think about what I had told him and to come back when I had.'

Immacolata made an angry grunting noise and crossed herself, then bellowed, 'Don Ambrogio!'

The priest appeared remarkably quickly, as though he was accustomed to being summoned and knew better than to leave his formidable housekeeper waiting.

'Don Ambrogio! I *told* you that boys had been in the church and why I knew it was boys, didn't I? You've even seen for yourself that the mark in the confessional goes all the way up the wall. I even told you who I thought it might be who done it!'

'Indeed you did,' he replied, looking at me quizzically, obviously trying to work out why I was in his kitchen and why I was so excessively bandaged.

Immacolata hadn't finished. Furiously, she demanded: 'So why did you not say anything about it when that brute Virgola came here with this poor child?'

'I did ask Graziella whether anybody else was involved and I gave her more than one opportunity to amend her story. I also asked her to go and think about it.'

'*Go and think about it?* And in the meantime you put her in the hands of that beast Virgola? Look what he's done to her, the sadist! She's been beaten! *Beaten!*'

'Maestro Virgola beat you?' Don Ambrogio was obviously taken aback. 'Because you took the blame for the incidents in the church?'

I nodded as I felt my eyes well again.

'Oh dear,' he said, rubbing his pink chins.

'*Oh dear?*' exclaimed Immacolata angrily, her face turning from red to crimson. 'Is that all you have to say, Don Ambrogio? *Oh dear?* That teacher comes marching into your house bandying blame and accusations at this innocent little girl and you said nothing? You *knew* it couldn't have been her!'

'Well, I did say we should be slow to chide.'

'And as for them boys, they're the same ruffians I caught putting ink in the holy water! Them very same boys that you won't have in your catechism classes.'

'Yes. Indeed. Pietro and Paolo.'

Immacolata rounded on Don Ambrogio with her hands on her hips

'You have dealt with this very badly, Don Ambrogio!' she said fiercely, wagging a fat finger at him. 'Your problem is, you're all long words and no common sense. Now, do something useful and find somebody to take poor little Graziella home. She can't walk in her current state. Call on somebody with a car and make sure she finishes her cake. I'll be back in a bit.'

'Where are you going?' he asked.

'To the school. To do what I cannot rely on you to do!' She slapped her cauliflower hat onto her head and left the priest's house with an air of absolute purpose.

*

It was Rita who gave me a report of what occurred next. Maestro Virgola had been furious that both Miracolino and I had run out of school. The class had been particularly quiet and Maestro Virgola had patrolled the aisles between the desks, grunting from time to time. He had not struck anyone else, but everybody had done their best to ensure he had no reason to. Rita said that even Pietro and Paolo had looked worried.

Then suddenly, Immacolata had marched into the classroom, surprising everybody, including Maestro Virgola.

'Could I ask you to wait outside, Signora Ogli? Class is in session.'

Clearly Immacolata had no intention of waiting outside.

'Perhaps I should expect a thrashing with that ruler of yours for having intruded?' she said. 'If you're willing to hit children, then you're probably willing to hit an old woman too. How dare you hit these children! And *how dare* you inflict violence on an innocent little girl?'

'An innocent girl? If it is the Ponti girl to whom you are referring, I will have you know, Signora Ogli, that the girl admitted everything, not just to me, but to the whole class and to Don Ambrogio,' he said self-righteously.

'Of course she did – she was frightened! But even if she had done it, it was not your business or your duty to punish her. It was absolutely nothing to do with you!'

Maestro Virgola puffed his chest out and replied, 'How I choose to discipline my class is my business entirely, Signora. But if you wish to discuss this with me in a civilised manner, then we can arrange a time, but this is neither the time nor–'

'Civilised? *Civilised*? Do you call beating little girls *civilised*? Hitting children is not acceptable under any circumstances. Do you think this is how children learn? Through fear and the threat of violence?' She looked at him with loathing. 'Have we not had enough of violence? We have lived through two wars! We should be educating our children with kindness and love. I have raised thirteen children, Maestro, and I have never raised my hand in anger against any of them – not even them what deserved it. You are a bully, a tyrant and a brute. And if you feel you have to resort to physical violence, you are obviously too incompetent to teach. And God help me, I will make it my personal crusade to make sure that you are removed from your position. And quickly!'

She crossed herself fervently several times, then jabbed her finger at Pietro and Paolo.

'As for you two,' she said, 'you can come with me!'

Class was dismissed with immediate effect.

*

Don Ambrogio arranged for me to be taken home in a car, as Immacolata had instructed. As I was waiting for my lift to arrive, Salvatore turned up with Miracolino, who had run home for help. Somehow he had managed to explain everything that he had witnessed. He had been in the church the entire time.

Although I did feel some sense of relief, I was still plagued by the thought of Pietro and Paolo exacting revenge by spreading the rumour about my aunt. I asked Salvatore to repeat everything that Miracolino had said to him, which he did. There was no mention of my aunt or the poisoning. The report ended with the desecration of the confessional.

My parents were horrified at the way I had been punished. My father was distraught.

'If I was an able-bodied man I'd whip that teacher within an

115

inch of his life,' he said to my mother. 'And then I'd whip him again. And once more, just to make sure.'

I was exonerated of all wrong-doing, relieved of all my chores, laid out on my father's bed in the corner of the kitchen and given yet more cake. My father pulled up a chair, sat by my side and offered to tell me a story, but I was so exhausted by my misadventures that I fell asleep before he could begin.

A nightmare woke me with a start sometime in the middle of the night. I had dreamed about opening the confessional door and finding my mother shackled to the seat begging to be saved. It took me a moment to realise I was still in my father's bed. He was sitting slumped and snoring in the chair beside me. He had not wanted to disturb me.

I lay down and tried to fall back to sleep, but all I could think of was Pietro and Paolo's revenge. I was so filled with panic that I began to cry again. My sobbing woke my father.

'What is it, my little one?' he said. 'Are you in pain?'

Of all the people in my world, I knew my Papá was the only one to whom I could pour out my woes. After all, he was the one who had made me keep the secret.

'They know about Zia Mina,' I sniffled.

'What?'

'Pietro and Paolo know about Zia Mina.'

'What do they know, little one?'

'They know she poisoned the soldiers and they said they'd tell.'

My father rearranged himself awkwardly in his chair and reached out his hand to take mine. 'Is that what all this is about?' he said quietly.

'They swore that if I told anyone what they did, they'd tell everyone the secret. And then the police would come and get Zia Mina and she would go to prison and you and Mamma might go too. Is it true, Papá? Did Zia Mina really poison those soldiers? I don't want any of you to go to prison!'

My father took several deep breaths, as though he was going through his words in his head before speaking them out loud.

'My little one,' he said. 'War is a terrible thing and I pray every day that we will never see another one. Bad things happen during wars. Our little village experienced a terrible atrocity which brought the war right into our own home. But that madness is over now and everything that happened needs to be put aside and forgotten. As for those two nasty boys, ignore their threats. Nobody is going to give those two lying thugs the time of day.'

He squeezed my hand gently, but I still wasn't convinced.

'But if it's a secret, how do Pietro and Paolo know what happened? Who else knows what happened? What if they tell?'

'Let me tell you a story,' said my father, leaning forward in his chair so that our faces were close. 'Once upon a time in a village in Lombardy there lived a family of mice. They were happy little farm mice. They had plenty to eat, they played in the fields and slept in soft straw beds. They didn't have a care in the world.' My father paused, then lowered his voice. 'But one day a gang of big, nasty rats arrived on their farm. They ate all the corn and took over the cosy mouse nests, and the poor little mice were so frightened that they ran to hide in a drain. They were very scared, very cold and very, very hungry. One night, five little mice crept out of the drain to try to find some food. But the big, nasty rats saw them! Big rats can run much faster than little mice so they easily caught the mice and hung them up by their tails. It was a winter's night and the rats watched and laughed as the little mice froze to death.'

'The little mice died?' I gasped. My father's stories were always funny and uplifting. They never touched on death.

'Yes,' said my father solemnly. 'And in the morning when the Mamma mouse woke up and found her babies hanging dead by their tails her heart was broken. But the big rats just sneered and said that they would do the same to any other little mouse they caught.'

'Did they catch any more?'

'All the mice stayed hidden in the cold ditch, except the Mamma mouse. She crept into the farmer's larder and took bread and chunks of cheese and laid them out in a trail, knowing that the rats would soon smell the food and come to eat it. And sure enough, those greedy rats did smell the food and they followed the trail, gobbling up every morsel. And right at the end of the trail was the biggest piece of cheese. The rats rushed to get it, fighting with each other to be the first to wolf down the tasty morsel. But what they didn't know was that the piece of cheese had been balanced on some corn stalks and that those corn stalks had been placed over a very deep drain with steep, slippery sides and deep water at the bottom. As soon as all the heavy rats stepped onto the corn stalks, the stalks snapped and the rats all fell into the drain and drowned.'

'What happened to the mice?'

'The little mice were free to live their lives once more. Of course, they would always be sad that five of them had died. But nobody was sad that the big, nasty rats had died – and nobody was angry with the Mamma mouse for doing what she did.'

My father reached over and stroked my hair.

'So do you understand now why in bad situations sometimes bad things are done, my little one?' he said. I thought about the story and nodded.

'Zia Mina was very brave, like the Mamma mouse,' I said.

'That's right. And you've been very brave too,' replied my father. 'But put it all out of your head now, my little one, and try to get some sleep.'

I wriggled across the bed to make room for my father. He got in awkwardly, wincing as he positioned himself beside me. I fell asleep cradled in his arm with my head resting on his chest.

*

118

My parents refused to let me go to school until Maestro Virgola was removed and until my welts had healed. In a show of solidarity, Rita's parents also kept her at home. We felt like outlaws.

We were sent a new teacher. Maestra Asinelli was very young. She was newly-qualified and slightly nervous at first, but we all behaved well for her, such was our relief at Maestro Virgola having been removed. Even Pietro and Paolo did as she asked. I think that all the boys in the class were a little bit in love with her. I think I was too.

She pinned pictures of birds and flowers on the bare classroom walls, as well as a colourful number chart and a map of the world.

Learning was transformed. We sang our times-tables. We learned poems. We wrote stories and even drew pictures. There was no rapping of heads, crushing of hands or eating of soap. The ruler was only ever used for its intended purpose of measuring. Maestra Asinelli believed that praise was a better form of instruction than punishment, and she was right. We learned more with Maestra Asinelli in a week than we had with Maestro Virgola in six months.

She was kind to Miracolino. She sat him at the front of the class so that he could see the blackboard, and whenever a malodorous waft floated through the classroom, she made no fuss and would simply open a window without interrupting the lesson. In any case, his flatulence had become far less frequent. It was likely the fear of being hit, not bad fish, which caused it.

As for Pietro and Paolo, Immacolata demanded that they should pay for their waywardness. Not being a believer in corporal punishment, she ordered that they spend every afternoon for a month under the instruction of Don Ambrogio, who would tutor them rigorously in catechism and Bible studies. They must, she insisted, have the fear of God driven into them.

It was Immacolata's way of punishing not only Pietro and Paolo, but also Don Ambrogio.

CHAPTER 9

Although there had been no embroidery work for my mother during the war, it was not long after its end that things began to pick up. A gentleman with a haberdashery shop in Cremona came to our house regularly, bringing linens for her to work on.

She set aside a work area by the kitchen window and kept the space around it scrupulously clean. There she would sit for hours in deep and silent concentration, speaking only when strictly necessary as she focused on metre after metre of recurring pattern. For my mother the quiet, repetitive work resembled some kind of meditation.

One day in late July a young girl called Fiorella arrived at Paradiso.

'Signora Ponti,' she said, 'Signora Marchesini would like to see you about some work. She asks if you can come to Cascina Marchesini tomorrow afternoon.'

My mother looked up from the sea of bed-sheets which surrounded her and slipped her needle through the collar of her dress. I could see that she was pleased.

'Tell Signora Marchesini I shall be there at half past four, if that is convenient for her.'

Fiorella gave a sort of curtsey and nodded. 'She will be at home all afternoon. Come to the side door. Pull hard on the bell-rope.'

'Graziella,' said my mother, rubbing her neck and stretching her arms, 'I'd like you to come with me tomorrow. We'll take Zia Mina's bicycle. We can load it up and balance it between us.'

Cascina Marchesini was the largest farm in the area and had

been in the family for many generations. The Marchesinis were not like us, or like other people in the village. They were rich.

Signora Marchesini had a motor car. There were very few cars in the village then. It was not unusual to see an ex-military vehicle, or maybe a Fiat Topolino occasionally, but Signora Marchesini's sleek, ultramarine-blue Alfa Romeo was an extraordinary vision. Its engine made a roaring noise which announced its approach from far away. Rumour had it that she had been given it by Mussolini himself.

I had seen Signor Marchesini on his tractor going to market. Sometimes his son would ride along with him. He didn't go to my school in the village.

My father said their house was so big, it had its own church. To me, this made the family incredibly exotic and mysterious.

I was so excited that I irritated my mother all afternoon with questions about the Marchesinis, but as she was not native to Pieve Santa Clara she knew little about them, except for the fact that they had a very big house, lots of cows and lots of money. In the end, she sent me outside to play.

I bounded into Zia Mina's garden bursting with excitement.

'Zia Mina! Zia Mina! I'm going to Cascina Marchesini!' I exclaimed, hopping from foot to foot.

My aunt stopped what she was doing and scowled. 'What would you want to go there for?'

'Signora Marchesini has some work for Mamma and I'm going to help carry it and we're going to see their house and they have a church and lots of cows and I hope I see the tractor and perhaps I'll even have a ride on it! Have you ever been to Cascina Marchesini? What's it like? Have you seen their church? Is it as big as our church in the village?'

My aunt raised her hands to hush me.

'I've no interest in that place,' she said curtly. 'And I certainly have no interest in those Marchesini people.'

With that, she waved me away.

We set off the next day. My mother sat me behind her on the saddle and told me to hold on tight as we rode northwards in the direction of Mazzolo, over the bridge and across the canal.

The canal's heyday was long past. Decades of neglect had left its waters dirty with effluent. Discarded items of scrap poked up above the waterline, bleeding their rust amongst the weed. I held my breath and buried my face in my mother's dress. The canal smelled like drains. Few houses along its banks were still inhabited. Miracolino's shack was just visible, buried beneath creepers and obscured by the long grass. The only sign of its inhabitants was a collection of tins and rags hanging from a scrubby tree.

The North Road sliced through the landscape, flanked by fields of sunflowers and maize. Two kilometres north of Paradiso was a turning, announced by two enormous brick columns. Once upon a time, long ago, they had been gateposts. The pins were still fixed into the mortar, but the gates were long gone. The columns were an incongruous sight, rising out of nowhere, standing like old, redundant sentries at the end of the road which led to Cascina Marchesini.

'Why are there gateposts and no gates, Mamma?' I asked.

'I expect the gates broke a long time ago,' she replied.

'But there are no walls or fences. Even if there were gates, you could just walk around the outside.'

'There must have been walls once, or hedges maybe.'

We made our way down a slender avenue of poplar trees. In the distance a series of long brick barns shimmered in the heat haze, their wide, arched openings like rows of huge black teeth. The avenue ended in a fork. The left-hand path led to the barns. The right-hand path was marked by two further gateposts, which were newer and far more ornate than those on the road. They were furnished with a set of elaborate iron gates which hung open, and beyond them swept a new avenue, edged with tightly-furled cypress trees.

We dismounted and proceeded through the gates on foot. As we rounded the curve of the driveway, the Marchesini house came into view.

I had never seen a more enormous, extravagant or embellished building, except perhaps for a church. It rose out of the flat farmland with an ostentatious presence, like a monumental terracotta-pink wedding cake. It was three storeys high, with a domed cupola and a turret. A fully grown man could have walked through its front door with another man standing on his shoulders.

In the very centre of the vast façade was the same coat of arms as on the church in the village. It depicted two long-legged birds facing one another. The tilt of their heads and the angle of their beaks formed a letter M.

'Be good,' warned my mother. 'If you're spoken to, answer politely. And speak in Italian. No dialect.'

As instructed, we made our way round the side of the house, past rows of white oleanders planted in colossal amphoral pots, to the rear door. My mother set the bicycle against the wall and pulled on the bell-rope as she kicked the dust off her shoes.

Fiorella answered the door. 'Signora Marchesini is waiting for you,' she said. 'Follow me.'

My mother and I were led through the kitchen and down a passageway to a grand oval hall. The gaze of numerous ancient portraits followed us. Feeling uneasy, I reached up and took my mother's hand.

Signora Marchesini was in the dining room standing beside a huge table. Its colossal legs were not much smaller in girth than me.

It was the first time I had seen Signora Marchesini at close quarters. She was extraordinarily beautiful. Her dress, which clinched around her waist and caressed her legs as she moved, was the same shade of red as her lipstick. She wore silk stockings and patent shoes with little block heels. I was mesmerised.

I wished that my mother could have such a lovely dress and shoes. I wondered how rich you had to be, to dress like that on an ordinary July afternoon, and whether Signora Marchesini had other, even more beautiful dresses. Perhaps she even had other pairs of shoes.

I could smell her too. She was encircled in an aura of rose, lily, face powder and other delicious scents which were unknown to me at that time, but which made me want to breathe the air around her and absorb her.

'Thank you for coming so promptly, Signora Ponti,' said Signora Marchesini. Even her voice was beautiful.

I was completely entranced and could not stop gazing at this vision of utter loveliness. She didn't acknowledge me at all.

My daze was broken by my mother. 'Graziella,' she said sharply. 'Don't stare.'

Signora Marchesini glanced at me, giving me the briefest but most intense of examinations.

'Would your daughter prefer to go outside?' she said in a tone which was more an instruction than a question.

'Go and play, Graziella. And don't get dirty,' said my mother.

I slipped out of the dining room, through to the oval hall and stood for a while, taking in my surroundings. A grand marble staircase curled all the way up to the first floor. I could see the sky through the glass cupola high above. I wondered where the Marchesinis' church was, thinking that as their house was so magnificent their church must be like a cathedral.

The garden was walled and laid out in a series of flowerbeds, lawns and paths with ornamental trees planted in symmetrical patterns. In its centre was a splendid fountain with spouts shaped like fish. It was unlike any garden I had ever seen. Our garden at

Paradiso smelled of tomatoes and soil. The Marchesini garden was an intoxicating mixture of floral scents, like Signora Marchesini's perfume.

I was barely a twenty-minute bicycle ride from my house, but Cascina Marchesini was a whole other world. I was so enthralled that in my distracted state I walked straight into Signor Marchesini.

'Good afternoon, young lady,' he said, catching me before I toppled backwards. 'What are you doing here?'

Signor Marchesini was very tall, even taller than Zia Mina. He was dressed in dirty work clothes and was carrying a writhing live rabbit by its back legs. I remembered my mother's instructions. Answer politely. No dialect.

'I am here with my mother to see Signora Marchesini about some work,' I said, craning my neck and squinting through the sun as the rabbit tried to kick itself free of Signor Marchesini's grasp.

'Ah, you're Luigi Ponti's little girl. What's your name?'

'Graziella.'

He stooped down, bowed his head and took my hand. 'It's a pleasure to meet you, Signorina Ponti. Amilcare Marchesini at your service.'

I had never had my hand shaken, let alone been addressed as 'Signorina'. I wasn't sure whether anyone had ever been at my service. I didn't know what I was supposed to say in return. The first thing that came into my head was, 'It's a pleasure to be in your garden, Signor Marchesini.'

Amilcare Marchesini laughed and I thought that I had said something wrong, but he replied, 'Thank you. It's very sweet of you to say so.'

'It's not like our garden. Our garden's full of vegetables. And we don't have a fountain.'

'We have vegetables too, just not in this part of the garden.'

I hoped I could have a look. I presumed that as everything at

125

Cascina Marchesini was so enormous their vegetable garden must be filled with gigantic vegetables.

'Do you know my son, Gianfrancesco?' asked Signor Marchesini and I replied, very politely, that I did not.

'He's in the plum orchard. Run along and find him. He'll probably be glad of the company.' Then Signor Marchesini patted my head, turned and sauntered back towards the house, whistling and swinging the struggling rabbit in his hand.

The orchard stretched out a long way on the other side of the garden wall. The tractor was parked in its centre, its trailer stacked with full crates – but there was no sign of Gianfrancesco Marchesini, just half a dozen fat red chickens pecking at the grass.

I went to inspect the plums to see whether they were bigger than normal plums, but they were of ordinary size. The dust on their purple skins turned them a curious shade of blue against the sunlight. They did look really good. I was tempted to taste one, but knew better than to do it without permission.

Suddenly a boy with skinny brown legs dropped down from a tree.

'Hello,' he said. 'Are you lost?'

'I was sent to look for Gianfrancesco Marchesini.'

He grinned. 'Well, you've found him. How can I help you?'

'I don't know,' I shrugged. 'Perhaps I could help *you*?'

I took my position at the foot of a tree while Gianfrancesco climbed back up and passed plums down to me. I would have climbed up too, but whenever I climbed Zia Mina's trees to gather fruit, I would tuck my skirt into my knickers. I knew it wasn't polite to let a boy see my knickers.

'How old are you?' I asked as I began filling the crates.

'Eleven years old. I will be twelve on the fifth of December. And you?'

'Nine and a half. I will be ten next March.' Despite being only two years older than me, Gianfrancesco seemed very grown up.

126

'Do you go to school?' I asked.

'Of course. I go to school in Cremona,' he replied.

'That's a long way to go.'

'It's less than an hour on the train, but I board there in the week.'

'Why don't you go to school in the village? It's much closer.'

'My parents want me to have a good education.'

I considered this, wondering how much better than Maestra Asinelli's classes a school in Cremona could be. Perhaps it was a school especially for rich people. Perhaps rich people needed to learn different things. There were so many questions that I wanted to ask. I began with, 'Have you got a lot of cows?'

'About three hundred at the moment, I think. Do you have cows?'

'No,' I replied. 'We're not rich.'

'We're not rich either,' he laughed. 'My parents have never got any money.'

I hoped that they would have enough money to pay my mother for her work, but thought that if they didn't, perhaps Signora Marchesini could give my mother her dress instead.

'Do you have your own church?' was my next question.

'My own church? Oh, well, yes. We have a chapel, but we don't use it any more.'

'Why not?'

'My father's an atheist. There hasn't been a service in the chapel since my grandfather's day. I can show you, if you like. Would you like a guided tour?'

I wasn't sure what an atheist was, nor had I any idea of what a guided tour might be, but I replied that I would like one very much.

'Great!' Gianfrancesco seemed pleased. 'But I promised my father I'd take the plums down to the store. Do you want to ride on the tractor with me?'

I could have danced around the orchard, such was my delight at the prospect of riding on the tractor. Although I wasn't sure whether my mother would allow it, I replied that I would without hesitation.

'Can you drive?' I asked.

'I can drive the tractor,' replied Gianfrancesco. 'My father only lets me drive it here on the farm though. I'm not allowed on the road. I'm going to learn to drive the car as soon as I can reach the pedals.'

My excitement must have been evident as I clambered up behind Gianfrancesco. Standing behind the driver's seat on a little platform I felt like a giant, perched so high up. My head was level with the tops of the plum trees and I could see over the hedges to the pastures beyond, where a herd of brown cows was grazing.

'Hold on tight,' said Gianfrancesco. 'It can get a bit bumpy.'

As the tractor chugged into life it almost shook me off the platform. Gianfrancesco was right. It was bumpy. We bounced across the orchard and down a gravel track, churning up great clouds of dust, much of which I swallowed because I couldn't stop grinning.

The farm buildings were almost as grand as the house and of equally gargantuan proportions. They were arranged in a quadrangle around a wide sandy yard, each with a covered portico in front, like a cloister. As we came to a halt, several workers appeared and set about unloading the crates.

Although the buildings were old, inside they were equipped with modern machinery. We passed a milking parlour where cows were lined up in booths attached to hoses and pumps. I stood by the open door, transfixed.

'What do you do with all your milk?' I asked.

'We sell some fresh and make cheese with the rest. Come and see if you like.'

At the far end of the quadrangle was a two-storey barn, where great wheels of golden cheese were laid out on wooden shelves. Hams hung drying from the beams.

I gazed along the lines of cheeses. They were stacked five shelves high. I tried to count them by singing my times-tables in my head, but there were just too many. The savoury smell of wood infused with centuries of maturing meats and cheeses made my stomach rumble very loudly. I was embarrassed, but Gianfrancesco laughed.

'Sounds as though you're hungry,' he said. 'I've got bread and cheese and a bottle of lemonade. Would you like some?'

We sat leaning against the barn wall in the cool shade, sharing Gianfrancesco's bread and cheese with a side order of plums. I had never tasted lemonade before. I was expecting it to be sour, but just like everything else at Cascina Marchesini, it was wonderful. I decided that I liked Gianfrancesco very much. He wasn't like the boys at school.

Eventually we meandered our way back to the house, stopping to drink at the fountain. My mother and Signora Marchesini were still busy inspecting linens and didn't notice us as we passed the dining room and crossed the oval hall. At its far end was the chapel door. It took some force to push it open.

The chapel was not like a cathedral. It was quite small and there was little to indicate its original use. The pews had been pushed aside to make space for an enormous quantity of stored furniture. Tables were stacked on tables. Chests were balanced on dressers and sideboards. Crates were piled three or four high. The altar was banked up with chairs, their upturned legs strung with spiders' webs. Boxes of ornaments, clocks and candlesticks fuzzed with dust covered every surface.

It was not a pleasant space. There was an acrid, unventilated smell to it, like bad breath.

'A lot of this furniture came from a castle near Ferrara,' said Gianfrancesco. 'Some of it is over five hundred years old. We've got even more stored upstairs. My grandfather won the castle and all its contents in a card game.'

'You have a castle too?'

'No. Unfortunately he lost the castle in the next game. But he kept the furniture. He nearly lost this house a few times. I'm glad he didn't. My grandfather was infamous.'

'What does that mean?'

'It means he was famous, but for bad reasons.'

'What reasons?'

'My father says he was drunk all the time. He made bad decisions. He closed the dairy farm and set up other businesses, but they all failed. He didn't look after the house either – and he gave a lot of our money to the church here. There's a picture of him here somewhere.'

Gianfrancesco disappeared behind a stack of tables and reappeared dragging a painting which was over twice his height and shrouded in a mesh of cobwebs

'Allow me to introduce my infamous grandfather, Carlo Marchesini,' he said with a grin and a theatrical gesture of his hand.

The portrait of Carlo Marchesini was much larger than life-size and showed a huge, fat man in high-waisted pantaloons and a red jacket, holding a brace of pheasants. Cascina Marchesini and the church of Pieve Santa Clara were in the background. The portrait was painted from an odd angle, as though the painter had been seated too low. Carlo Marchesini's head was held high and I could see up his nostrils. He was quite literally looking down his nose at me.

'I don't know what my grandparents looked like,' I said. 'We don't have any paintings at our house. We have a photograph of the Pope, but we're not related to him.'

We stood contemplating the portrait of Carlo Marchesini until from somewhere in the distance I heard my mother calling my name.

'I have to go,' I said.

'That's a shame,' replied Gianfrancesco. 'I haven't been able to show you the rest of the house. But you can come back here whenever you want.'

'Can I?'

'Yes. I would like that very much.'

I was thrilled.

Neither my mother nor Signora Marchesini were in the dining room. We hurried back through the kitchen and out through the side door where Signor Marchesini was standing leaning against a column eating apricots. The rabbit, now no longer alive, was hanging by its heels from a hook.

'Your Mamma's looking for you,' he said as he dug the stone from an apricot with his penknife and ate the fruit in one mouthful. 'But before you go, make sure you take some of our cheese. 'Cesco, go and cut a nice big slab for Graziella to take home.'

My new friend raced off and soon reappeared with a wrapped package, which I took from him.

'Thank you,' I said, then repeated it twice more, just to make sure I was being polite.

'Our pleasure,' replied Signor Marchesini, winking.

I had heard my mother say to my father that rich people were not very nice, but Signor Marchesini seemed extremely kind.

Eventually my mother was ushered out by Fiorella.

'Good afternoon, Signora Ponti,' said Signor Marchesini, doffing his straw hat.

My mother lowered her eyes and did not reply, which I thought was curious as I had been ordered to speak when spoken to.

'Hurry, Graziella,' she said, 'or we won't be eating until nine o'clock. I didn't realise we had been here so long. The clock in the house says it's nearly half past six.'

'Would you like me to run you back home in the car?' asked

131

Signor Marchesini, putting his hat back on. At this point I thought I might explode with excitement.

'Thank you,' replied my mother, 'but I wouldn't wish to trouble you. Anyway, I would have to come back for my bicycle. And it's such a nice afternoon – the walk will be good for us. Your wife kindly offered to drop off the material tomorrow, so we don't have anything heavy to carry.'

'As you wish,' said Signor Marchesini, tipping his hat deferentially with his index finger.

My mother blushed and also said, 'Thank you,' three times. I tried not to show I was disappointed.

We made our way back down the avenue of cypress trees as their shadows lengthened. My mother seemed preoccupied. As we passed the sentinel gateposts I imagined her in Signora Marchesini's red silk dress, and how it would flutter as she walked. Today she was wearing a yellow cotton dress, which she had made herself and embroidered with tiny cross-stitched flowers on the breast pocket.

'I love it here,' I said. 'Gianfrancesco was really nice.'

There had been something about him which I could not quite put my finger on, but as I thought about my time with him, it came to me.

'He reminded me of Ernesto,' I said.

'Really?'

'Yes. Except he wasn't naughty. And he said I can come back whenever I want.'

'Did he?'

'Yes. So can I?'

'We'll see.'

'They have a lovely house. They do have their own church and lots of furniture which came from a castle. And they have a barn full of cheese.' I brandished the package.

'Some people have too much,' said my mother, and withdrew back into her own thoughts.

I withdrew into mine, suspecting that perhaps I had fallen a little bit in love with Gianfrancesco Marchesini.

CHAPTER 10

My father was delighted with the cheese. He rubbed his hands together in anticipation as my mother laid out our supper.

'That was very generous of Marchesini,' he said. 'That's an expensive piece of cheese there.'

'Expensive for people like us,' muttered my mother.

'I hear they've mechanised everything,' continued my father. 'Pozzetti said they have machines for everything, even milking. I can't imagine how the cows deal with that. Apparently their dairy is like a laboratory. Marchesini even had it inspected by the sanitation department and they gave him a certificate. Pozzetti said that they're producing more cheese than they ever did, but they only need a fraction of the workforce because they have so many machines.'

'That's not good for the farmworkers,' said my mother. 'That's only good for Marchesini's pocket.'

'It's going the way of everything,' sighed my father. 'It's progress.'

'Progress?' my mother said irritably. 'How can it be progress if people can't work and feed their families?'

'They have to find other work elsewhere.'

'There'll be nobody left in the countryside in twenty years' time. Just machines.'

'Ah, but somebody will have to make the machines. The farmworkers can move to the cities and find jobs in the factories.'

My mother shook her head and tutted.

'You've never been to a city,' she said. 'Cities are grim and dirty and full of miserable people. I'd rather be a poor farm labourer than a poor factory worker, that's for sure.'

That evening, we all feasted. Mamma had made Papá's favourite dish of frittata with zucchini. He cut off a piece of the cheese we'd been given, grated it over his supper and sliced it onto his bread. Once he had scraped the rind with his teeth, he took the hard outer crust and placed it in a cup of hot water.

'That should soften up nicely for my breakfast,' he said. 'It's the best cheese I've tasted for years.'

My mother said he had been greedy, but he just patted his full belly and burped.

I was tucked into bed shortly after. My mother kissed my forehead.

'Be good. Go to sleep, and stay on your own side,' she said.

I nestled down into the cool sheets, but I had no intention of falling asleep. The only reason I ever looked forward to bedtime was because I could eavesdrop on my parents' conversations in the kitchen. It was a time for gossip, exchanges of news and opinions, and a time when I could learn things not meant for my ears.

'Did Signora Marchesini give you a lot of work?' I heard my father ask.

'Yes. She has some antique table linen and ten sets of bedding which she wants repaired, washed and pressed. Most of the bedding is silk. It must have cost a fortune.'

'It's probably Marchesini silk. The Marchesinis used to farm silkworms.'

'Silkworms? Here in Lombardy?'

'Yes. It was one of Carlo Marchesini's big ideas.'

'Who's Carlo Marchesini?'

'Amilcare Marchesini's father. He's long gone now, but he thought there was more money to be made out of silk than there was out of milk. It worked for a while. The Marchesinis farmed the worms in one of those buildings you can see from the road. They had everything there – the farm, the processing plant. They used to grow mulberry bushes on their land to feed them.'

'So what happened? Why did they stop?'

'The silkworms caught a disease – some kind of atrophy. Everything stopped very suddenly. One moment it was a thriving business with dozens of jobs, the next it was closed. It was quite a blow for Carlo Marchesini. It hit him very hard.'

'I expect it hit the workers harder,' said my mother. 'Rich people always stay rich.'

'Well, I don't know how rich they are now.'

'Don't be ridiculous! That house, all that land, the furniture alone must be worth a fortune.'

'I don't know if they have a lot of actual money,' said my father. 'I have heard a few people say that they struggle. All that new-fangled dairy machinery was paid for with a loan from the bank. I don't think they make much from the cheese. Just because you have a big farm doesn't mean a big income. Think of all the expenses.'

'They don't seem short of money to me. Signora Marchesini was wearing a very lavish dress.'

'I think that Signora Marchesini is Signor Marchesini's biggest expense,' my father said, sounding amused.

'I don't think she liked me,' my mother told him.

'What makes you say that?'

'She looked at me as though I wasn't up to her standards.'

'Don't let that worry you. She looks down that elegant nose at everybody. But Amilcare Marchesini's always been well-liked. He's a good sort. Down to earth. He works the farm with the labourers and doesn't mind getting his hands dirty. The same couldn't be said for his father though.'

'Why?'

'He was a drunk. He used to ride around on a big chestnut horse as though he was the King of Italy. He was a womaniser too. Carlo Marchesini had a string of young mistresses. His liking for the ladies got him into trouble many times.'

There was silence for a moment, then I heard my father chuckle and say, 'Carlo Marchesini was shot in the arse.'

'In the war?'

'No,' laughed my father. 'It happened like this. At one point he was involved with a baker's daughter. He used to visit her in the early hours of the morning when he knew her father would be occupied in the bakery. But one night the baker came home early and heard you-know-what going on upstairs. Carlo Marchesini puffing like a train, the daughter howling like a she-wolf.'

'Hush,' hissed my mother. 'Graziella will hear you.'

My father lowered his tone. I lifted my head and strained my ears.

In a low, conspiratorial whisper, he went on, 'So the baker takes his shotgun, goes running up the stairs and into the bedroom. By this time Carlo Marchesini has jumped out of the window and is running across the garden half-naked. The baker takes aim and shoots him – gets him right on the bare arse! They say Carlo's wife had to dig out the lead shot with a knife and that one of his buttocks looked like the skin of an orange until the day he died.'

'His poor wife,' I heard my mother say. 'If I'd been humiliated like that I'd have been tempted to use that knife very differently.'

'I'll bear that in mind the next time I go womanising,' replied my father, and I heard the sound of a slap.

'The boy, Gianfrancesco, seemed nice,' said my mother after a while. 'He looked after our Graziella.'

'I haven't seen him for a long time, but last time I did he looked exactly like his father did at the same age. Lean and lanky with arms and legs like over-cooked spaghetti. But he'll fill out. All the Marchesini men end up tall.'

'Of course they do,' said my mother. 'Generations fed on good food and plenty of it. I don't suppose their forefathers starved, like ours did.'

There was a pause. When my mother spoke again her tone was perplexed. 'What's Mina got against the Marchesinis? When I went to borrow her bicycle she was quite peculiar with me.'

'What do you mean by peculiar?'

'It seemed to put her in a very bad mood. I know she has her moods, but she'd been fine until I told her where I was going. She just stomped off and closed herself in the house.'

'Mina grew up at Cascina Marchesini. Her mother was a silk-worker there.'

This astounding revelation made me sit up. I felt a pang of jealousy that Zia Mina had grown up in a place which I thought to be so wonderful, and I could not think of any reason why anybody would not love it. I tried hard, but couldn't catch what my father was telling Mamma. Whatever it was, it took some time to explain and it made her gasp.

'What!' she exclaimed.

'Mina's ashamed,' my father replied, more clearly now.

'Graziella said something as we were leaving.'

'What was that?'

'She said that the Marchesini boy reminded her of Ernesto.'

'And what did you think?' my father asked. 'Was he anything like Ernesto?'

'I couldn't say. I barely saw him.'

After those words, I must have fallen asleep – and so I heard no more.

*

Signora Marchesini dropped off her items the following day. She parked her Alfa Romeo by the gate. It was a thing of beauty, with an enormously long bonnet and elegant running boards. It made a gurgling sound as its engine cooled.

I watched as Signora Marchesini trod carefully across the yard.

Today she was wearing a green floral dress, different shoes and a wide-brimmed hat, worn at an angle. It was held in place with a pearl hatpin.

'Good afternoon, Signora Ponti,' she said. 'I have the linens in the car. Would you come to fetch them?'

'Graziella!' called my mother. 'Come and help.'

Signora Marchesini didn't carry anything. She stood by the open door of her car and watched us unload, then followed us over to the house and waited on the step as we piled the packages onto the trestle table which my mother had erected especially.

'Won't you come in?' said my mother.

'Thank you, but I must get home. Can I remind you to deal with the white and yellow set first? That is the only one which is urgent.'

'Of course. I can have it ready by the end of the week.'

'If I am not at home, you can leave it with my domestic girl, Fiorella.'

'Don't you wish to collect it?' asked my mother hopefully, casting her eye over the enormous quantity of bedlinen.

'I am very busy, Signora Ponti. It would be best if you could deliver it.' The woman then turned to leave, tip-toeing through the gravel to protect her heels, the pearl on her silver hatpin flashing in the sun.

As the car pulled away, my mother said scornfully, 'Very busy, indeed! I would love to be as *busy* as her. She has a car and all day to do nothing at all, but is quite happy for me to have to get on my bicycle to deliver her spare sheets.'

Although I could understand my mother's point, I was pleased. That meant I could go back and see Gianfrancesco.

So excited was I about going to deliver the linen that I checked on my mother's progress and counted the days. In my mind, visiting Cascina Marchesini was like visiting a foreign country, with a different language and customs. I had enjoyed my afternoon with Gianfrancesco so much that I could think of little else but going back.

'Mamma, can I help you with your work?' I enquired, thinking that the sooner the sheets were repaired, the sooner we could go back to deliver them.

'Help me? This is work I'm to be paid for, Graziella. It's not something you can do.'

I had often played at sewing before on little scraps of cotton cloth, making irregular stitches in an attempt to form patterns and flowers, but my childish attempts bore no resemblance to my mother's expert embroidery work.

'Can't you teach me? Please, Mamma?'

My mother was surprised at my keenness, but not displeased, although she had no idea as to my motives.

'All right,' she said, 'but you must concentrate. And whatever task I give you, you must complete it. I won't spend time teaching you for you to run off to play after ten minutes because you're bored.'

I promised that I would be an exemplary student. For my first lesson my mother drew straight lines in pencil on a cotton off-cut, which I was expected to embroider neatly with lines of running stitches of equal length. She let me choose any colour of thread I wanted. I chose a vivid pink.

'Watch carefully and pay attention,' she said, wetting one end of the thread between her lips and passing it through the eye of the needle. 'You have to learn to rely on both your hands. One hand stays on one side of the fabric, the other on the other. Push the needle down through the fabric nice and straight. Leave enough tail on the thread to wrap your next stitches around it because you can't tie knots. Your work must look the same on both sides of the fabric.'

I did as instructed, but it was not as easy as my mother made it look. In fact, it wasn't easy at all. I stabbed my needle upwards several times, missing the line each time. When I finally pierced the line, the stitch was too long, but after a period of trial and error, my hands grew accustomed to the feel of the needle and thread, and by the end of the morning I had produced a respectable selection of straight lines and lattice patterns. My mother inspected the work on both sides and seemed quite pleased.

Before long I could do running stitches in lines, curves and even more complex patterns. Once my mother was satisfied that I was competent enough, she taught me backstitch, split stitch, stem stitch and chain stitch. By this time I was eager to work on the Marchesini linens, but my mother still refused. Instead she suggested that I should try embroidering a handkerchief.

'Try this one,' she said, pointing to a daisy motif in her sketch book, a simple combination of stem and chain stitch, but I had more ambitious ideas. I decided upon a cherry blossom design which I had seen my mother embroider on an antimacassar. I liked it because of the rich crimson and pink blossoms and the deep brown crooked bough.

'That one is far too difficult for a first attempt,' she said.

'Please Mamma, let me try.'

She considered this for a moment, then said, 'If you start this, Graziella, I will expect it to be finished, and finished well. Are you sure?'

Embroidery made my neck and shoulders ache and my eyes grow tired, but I thought it best not to complain. It taught me great respect for my mother's craft, for her concentration and her stamina. It also made me understand her insistence on pristine hands and a clean work area. When I'd finished, the only thing I was scolded for was the shadow of a thumb-print on the edge of my handkerchief.

My mother was evangelical about cleanliness around her work. She steered clear of anything which might sully her fingers, such as working in the garden or chopping onions, and regularly soaked her fingers in lemon juice to bleach out any stains and neutralise unpleasant odours.

My cherry blossom handkerchief took far longer than I imagined it would. In my mother's experienced hands, it would have been completed in a few hours. In my amateur, fumbling fingers it took nearly three days, but I was determined to do a good job.

The finished result passed my mother's inspection with very little criticism, which was in itself praise enough. My father, on the other hand, applauded my work extravagantly as I presented my precious handkerchief before him on the table.

'How lovely!' he exclaimed, then turned to my mother and said, 'This is very good. How your work is improving, my dear.'

My mother did not take part in the joke.

'It was me who made it, Papá,' I said.

He gave a loud, theatrical gasp. *'You?'*

'Yes, Papá.'

'No, it's impossible. How can it be? There isn't a little girl in the whole world who could make something as beautiful as this.' He clapped his hands in joy. 'How clever you are! I am so proud. Those cherries look so good I could eat them.'

*

The day before we were due to return to Cascina Marchesini I awoke to the sound of loud, excited chatter in the yard outside. I knew it was very early as the dawn chorus was in full voice and the light glinting through the gaps in the shutters was dim. There was a strong burning smell in the air. My mother was not in bed. Most mornings I was aware of her getting up. I would roll over into the imprint of her body and burrow into the warmth, but that morning when I reached across, the dent left by her body was cold. I sat up, trying to discern the conversations being had outside.

I found my mother, my father and my aunt in the yard, still in their nightshirts. Pozzetti, Salvatore and several men from the village had gathered around them. The burning smell was intense.

'What's happened?' I asked.

'A train has come off the tracks,' my aunt explained, 'and it's on fire.'

A freight train carrying tobacco had been ambushed just outside Mazzolo. One of the robbers had fired a shot to scare the driver, and a spark from the bullet had set the cargo, which was by definition highly flammable, alight. Nobody had been hurt, but the train had derailed.

News of the calamity had spread as quickly as the thick cloud of smoke, and within the hour men and boys from all the adjoining villages had raced to salvage what they could. Pozzetti set off on his bicycle. Instead of carrying my father, today the trailer was piled high with sacks and boxes.

I don't believe I had ever seen a policeman in the village before that day, but suddenly they were everywhere. I stood by the gate with my father and Salvatore, watching as police bicycles, motorcycles and other vehicles streamed back and forth. It was not long before we had news that there had been arrests, not of the robbers who had held up the train, but of local men and boys who had gone to loot it.

My mother said she was glad my father was not able to go. Rita's mother, who had also heard news of the arrests, was tight-lipped. She stood in our yard, balancing a baby on her hip, and said that if her husband was arrested, she would skin him alive.

Pozzetti returned later that morning. Fortunately, he had not been caught. With him, he brought a bag of tobacco for my father: it was a kind gift, albeit an impractical one as Papá did not smoke.

'We can sell it,' said my mother.

'And who do you think will buy it?' my father replied. 'Everyone has sacks of the stuff now. The whole region will be smoking for free for years.'

'So what are you going to do with it?'

'I'm going to smoke it myself.'

'But you don't smoke.'

'Only because we can't afford it. It's not because I don't want to.'

'It's a wretched habit and it can't be good for you. People who smoke get coughs.'

'My dear, considering everything else I have to deal with, a little cough is not going to bother me. Anyway, it only causes a cough because it clears the lungs.'

'Well, you'll have to smoke outside. I don't want you stinking out the house with it, especially with all those fine Marchesini linens in there.'

And so my father was exiled to a bench outside my aunt's kitchen. I watched as he sat in a grey cloud, spluttering and spitting, alternating between drags of his inexpertly-rolled cigarettes and sips of medicine. My mother locked the door and would not let him in until he stripped off outside and hung his clothes in a tree, where they stayed all night.

By the end of the week my mother had repaired the embroidery and laundered two sets of sheets and a tablecloth. She wrapped them carefully in brown paper and secured the parcel to my aunt's bicycle with string.

We set off along the road, balancing the bicycle between us. The smell of burning tobacco still hung in the air and intensified as we approached Cascina Marchesini.

My mother rang at the side door, as before. Fiorella opened it immediately.

'I am returning some of the Signora's linens,' announced my mother.

Fiorella gestured for us to come in and said, 'Wait here.'

After a few minutes, Signora Marchesini appeared. This time she was wearing a pale blue dress, fastened around her wasp waist with a broad satin sash. She had on yet another pair of shoes.

'Good afternoon, Signora Ponti.'

'There are two bedding sets,' said my mother. 'The yellow set, as you requested, and another set with little lilac flowers. And the linen tablecloth. All repaired, laundered and pressed.'

'Thank you for being so prompt,' said Signora Marchesini. 'May I see, please?'

My mother opened out the brown paper and the delicate scent of soap burst forth.

Signora Marchesini inspected the embroidered edges carefully. 'Excellent,' she said at last. 'When will the other sets be ready?'

'I can have them all done within about three weeks.'

Signora Marchesini nodded and said, 'That would be perfect. I will see you in three weeks' time, Signora Ponti.'

My mother hesitated. 'When can I expect payment for the completed work?' she asked.

'I thought it would be when all the work was finished,' said Signora Marchesini. 'But if you are in need of money and wish me to pay as you finish each set, I can do so.'

'That would be preferable,' said my mother.

'Come back on Monday and I will have your money. If I am not here, I will leave it with Fiorella.'

We were ushered out briskly. My mother grabbed the bicycle and wheeled it off at some speed. I had to run to keep up.

'Monday!' she spat. 'I have to come all the way back here on Monday! She can collect the rest of her damned sheets when they're done. And she can bring the damned money with her!'

It was clear that my mother had no wish to speak on the way home. She cycled so fast that I do not know how I held on. I was deeply disappointed that I had not seen Gianfrancesco.

CHAPTER 11

Thanks to Salvatore's hard work at Paradiso, Zia Mina's vegetable garden had quadrupled in size and he had plans to extend it further the following season. The crops now no longer just fed us. There was a surplus to sell at the market. Before Salvatore's arrival my aunt's only income had been from renting out the fields behind Paradiso to a neighbouring farmer.

Salvatore had created cosy lodgings for himself. He had partitioned off a section of the barn under the old hayloft and acquired various items of furniture. Pozzetti had helped him to install a little stove so he could be warm in the winter.

Zia Mina allowed him to take a bath in her tub once a week, providing she was not home at the time. Salvatore's bath-times had to be arranged with prior consent and had to last no longer than an hour.

My aunt would always check that he was out of the bathroom and dressed before re-entering her house. Being on the same premises as a naked man, even if he was upstairs and completely out of sight, was too improper for her.

Salvatore would often tease Zia Mina about her prudishness. One particularly hot summer's day, he had removed his shirt and was busy working in the garden, stripped to the waist.

'Salvatore, I don't want you half-naked in my garden!' my aunt said.

'My apologies, Donna Mina. I didn't mean to offend you. Come and help me out of my trousers so I can be fully naked for you.'

My aunt told him to behave himself and poked him with the handle of her rake.

Salvatore's good humour rubbed off on Zia Mina. They had an affectionate respect for one another. Although they sometimes bickered light-heartedly, like an old married couple, there was never a truly irate word between them.

Salvatore would consult Zia Mina on any matter which he considered might require a woman's judgement, and my aunt sought and respected Salvatore's opinions on most subjects. Throughout her life she was prone to dark and melancholy moods, but he could lift her spirits in a way that nobody else seemed able to do. It was a mutually beneficial arrangement.

Salvatore still sang about Carmela, his old sweetheart. Her photograph was still his bookmark.

'How did you meet Carmela?' I asked.

'Her family ran a restaurant two streets away from mine in Naples and I'd seen her pass by my door many times carrying flowers,' he replied. 'But I was young and didn't have the courage to speak to her. Then one day I saw her outside the Church of Santa Maria del Carmine and she came to speak to me.' He shook his head. 'What a young fool I was. It turned out she had been going past my restaurant to try to attract my attention. The flowers were for the church. She would offer them to the Madonna del Carmine and pray that I would notice her. *Criatura*, I fell in love with her straight away, but I was too shy to tell her. We'd been meeting to talk for over a year when she said, "Salvá, what have I got to do to make you kiss me?" Well, all she had to do was to ask! And that was how our story started.'

The problem was that Carmela's family had never liked Salvatore's family and had been so disapproving of their relationship that they had threatened to kill him.

'In the end, they sent her away,' he said. 'One day she was there and the next she was gone.'

'Did you look for her?'

'Of course. I made inquiries, but nobody knew – and if they

did, they wouldn't say. And it was not long afterwards that my restaurant was bombed and I was left with nothing. Even if I had found her, I couldn't have given her a good life. But I was glad she wasn't in Naples when the bombs fell. Her family's restaurant was destroyed too and several of them were killed. I prayed she was somewhere out of harm's way. Perhaps it was for the best.' He sighed heavily. 'I think of her every day and I pray that she is happy. But I like to think that we are still connected in some way, so I pray to the Madonna del Carmine to keep her safe, and I hope that when my Carmela prays to the Madonna that perhaps from time to time she thinks of me too.'

*

Salvatore's swarthy southern looks and approachable demeanour meant that he was not without female admirers. Since his arrival at Paradiso he had attracted the amorous attentions of two ladies, Rosalina and Bianca.

My aunt sold her produce at the market in Pieve Santa Clara on a Tuesday and at the market in Mazzolo on a Thursday. Salvatore pushed the barrow of fruit and vegetables to and from each market and minded both stalls. He had caught Rosalina's eye in Pieve Santa Clara and Bianca's in Mazzolo.

Although Salvatore was not tempted by their advances, neither lady seemed willing to take no for an answer. He had expressed some relief that his two admirers lived in different villages and frequented different markets on different days. He said he feared that if they met, there would be ructions.

Rosalina was a wholesome girl with a pretty, gap-toothed smile and a mellifluous giggle. She smelled of soap and seemed to shine with cleanliness. Her clothes were always starched and pristine. She had replaced the laces of her boots with ribbons to match her hat, something which I thought was truly inspiring at the time.

Rosalina had taken to walking back from Pieve Santa Clara to Paradiso with Salvatore every market day. There was no reason for her to do this other than wanting his company. She lived on the other side of the village, where the North Road became the South Road. Accompanying Salvatore caused her a detour of over two and a half kilometres.

Every time they arrived at Paradiso I would watch her pause and linger in the hope that Salvatore would offer more than a courteous goodbye, but she would be left disappointed each time.

Bianca's method of trying to win Salvatore's affections was altogether more direct. She was conspicuously buxom and always wore clothing which displayed her ample assets, and it seemed that whenever Salvatore was near, her top buttons would pop open spontaneously. She would stand with her body arched suggestively and throw her head back as she laughed, flirted and chatted with Salvatore, who did his best not to be too distracted by her plentiful bosom, which spilled out over the top of her brassiere as though it was fighting to escape.

My father found Salvatore's predicament very amusing.

'That Bianca isn't leaving much to the imagination,' he said. 'The way she sticks those huge great breasts right under your nose, she'll have your eye out with her nipple if you're not careful.'

'I know, Don Luigi.' Salvatore looked sheepish. 'And the less I try to look, the closer they seem to get.'

My father chuckled and patted his shoulder. 'You're a gentleman, Salvatore,' he said.

'Either that or a fool,' Salvatore replied.

For a time neither woman knew that she had a rival, but gossip travels between villages. People had noticed Rosalina's walks with Salvatore and speculated on the possibility of a romance blossoming. The information had reached Bianca, who wasted no time in going to the market in Pieve Santa Clara to weigh up her adversary.

As Salvatore had feared, the meeting was not a friendly one. Bianca appeared wearing a particularly low neckline and eyed her competitor with contempt. Rosalina gave a similar look in return. The animosity was palpable.

Bianca leaned over a fruit stall, her shapely cleavage on show.

'These are beautiful melons, don't you think, Salvatore?' she said, running her fingertips sensuously over a display of cantaloupes.

'Yes. They're excellent,' Salvatore replied, swallowing hard.

'I would imagine that they're *very* sweet. Although of course it's impossible to tell until you taste them.' She kept her gaze fixed on Salvatore. 'And right now, they're fully in season,' she purred.

'But melons can be very disappointing,' Rosalina retorted. 'Over-ripe. Hollow inside. And eventually they turn to mush.'

The hostile meeting in the market escalated the rivalry.

In order to increase her chances Rosalina also began to walk back from church with Salvatore on Sundays. Her Sunday clothes were even more pristine than her ordinary clothes. As he did not have a barrow to push, she would link her arm through his.

However, one Sunday they arrived back together later than usual. Salvatore was looking flustered and Rosalina was unusually dishevelled. Her skirt was creased and muddied and her hair had fallen loose. My aunt raised an eyebrow, but Salvatore quickly explained that there had been an unfortunate accident and Rosalina had fallen over. She had grazed her knee and her elbow. He asked my aunt whether she would mind bathing the wounds and treating both with a dab of iodine.

It transpired that as they made their way towards Paradiso, Rosalina had surprised Salvatore by stopping suddenly and turning to invite a kiss, but Salvatore had not been paying attention. He had stumbled into her and knocked her into the ditch. The incident had left him mortified, but Rosalina was not deterred.

Bianca also intensified her efforts. My father commented that if her décolletages got any lower, Salvatore would be able to see her navel.

As neither woman was making any progress, they began to bring Salvatore gifts of food. He would arrive back from market with cakes, the little round flatbreads called *crescentine*, pots of pickles and jars of pesto.

'At this rate you'll never have to cook again, Salvatore,' my father said.

'Receiving gifts is an expensive business, Don Luigi,' Salvatore complained. 'I can't possibly take what they give me and give nothing back.'

He would give Rosalina and Bianca fruit and vegetables from Zia Mina's stall in return, but as they were not officially his to give, he would have to pay my aunt for what he took.

Eventually the two women concluded that their gifts of food were not doing the trick.

Rosalina knitted Salvatore a red hat with a matching scarf so that he could be warm when he minded the market stall on chilly days. She said that the colour brought out his dark eyes.

Not to be outdone, Bianca made him a cologne from rose water and geranium oil. She had insisted on dabbing it on his neck herself. My father said it made him smell like a tart's handkerchief, but Salvatore wore it throughout the summer, stating that it was an excellent mosquito repellent.

The situation had gone on for almost a year when one day, by chance, both women arrived at Paradiso unannounced and at precisely the same time. They approached from different directions and stopped simultaneously by the gate, where they eyed one another jealously as they asked for Salvatore.

'He's around here somewhere,' my aunt said. 'I saw him in the garden barely ten minutes ago, so he can't be far.'

She called for him repeatedly, but no answer came.

When neither lady showed any inclination to leave, my aunt finally said to me, 'Graziella, go and see if you can find Salvatore.'

I searched the house, the garden, the barn, the outbuildings, every place he was likely to be and every place he was unlikely to be, calling his name as loudly as I could, but there was no sign of him. He had vanished into thin air.

It was a full hour later, when my aunt had finally managed to convince Rosalina and Bianca to go on their way that I saw him peer down from the old hayloft. He had climbed up and pulled the ladder up behind him.

'What are you doing there?' I asked. 'We've been looking for you.'

'I know,' he replied. 'I was hiding.'

'Hiding?'

'I couldn't go down there with both those women looking for me. It could have been carnage.' He shuddered. 'Are you sure they've gone?'

'Yes. Zia Mina sent them away.'

Salvatore gave a sigh of relief, re-positioned the ladder and climbed back down.

'That was a close one,' he said.

'But why don't you like them, Salvatore? They like you a lot.'

'I know,' he said, picking bits of hay from his hair. 'It's not that I don't *like* them. I do like them. They're both lovely women, each in their own special way, but I don't feel anything beyond liking them. The thing is, when you've loved someone as I have, from the depths of your heart and your soul, and they've loved you back in the same way, anything else just seems like a pointless compromise.'

He and I walked slowly to the door of the barn. Before we left, he added: 'Maybe one day in the future, when I'm sitting all by myself as a lonely, childless old man I'll think back and realise I've been an idiot, but when you've known real love, it's like being used to eating *migliaccio* and *strufoli*, and then just being offered plain sponge cake.' Seeing my incomprehension he explained, 'Lemon cake with ricotta and honey balls. There's nothing wrong with plain sponge cake, *criatura*. It's delicious. But it's not *migliaccio* or *strufoli*.'

*

The incident with the two women had made Salvatore very thoughtful. Later that same day, he asked me, 'Have you heard of pizza, *criatura*?'

I said that I had not.

'It's very common in Naples. It's nothing more than flatbread, mozzarella cheese and tomato and anything else which is going spare. There are places in Naples which sell only pizza, by the slice if you want. People eat it in the streets. And I was thinking, if they can do it in Naples, why not here?'

'Here in Pieve Santa Clara?'

'I was thinking in Cremona. All those busy people would probably be thankful for a quick, hot meal. The thing is with pizza, even if you're not hungry, the moment you smell it, oh, then you really want it! But it needs to be cooked in a proper wood oven. It's just not the same if you cook it in a stove.'

Salvatore's words drifted into Neapolitan. He was talking more to himself than to me. The incident with Bianca and Rosalina seemed entirely forgotten. Later that day I found him with my father in the laundry room.

'We have one good back and three good hands between us, Don Luigi. We should be able to lay a few bricks,' he said.

'It's not as easy as that, Salvatore. We'd have to build a platform for your oven. And a proper flue. And building a domed structure is quite a process. We'd have to make up a profile – a supporting structure made of wood.'

Salvatore scratched his chin. 'Could we not ask Don Pozzetti to help us?'

Shortly afterwards, Pozzetti also joined them. The three men stood deep in conversation.

'What are you all plotting?' asked my mother, appearing in the doorway which led through to our kitchen.

'Salvatore wants to build an oven to cook his pizzas,' said my father.

'It's not real pizza if it hasn't been cooked in a wood oven,' said Salvatore.

Over the following days Pozzetti constructed an arched profile from pieces of scrap wood and an old door. My father and Salvatore set about gathering everything else they needed to construct his oven.

They collected and scavenged bricks from different places. There were several dozen which had been stacked in the barn since my father's accident. Pozzetti had a few dozen more. Salvatore, who had an uncanny talent for finding exactly what he needed when he needed it, managed to charm several people in the village into letting him have spare bricks in exchange for the promise of pizza once the oven was built.

The bricks were collected and stacked ready for work to start. My father counted, re-counted and calculated.

'They should be enough, just about,' he said. 'But we will have to be very careful with the cuts and hope we don't get too many breakages.'

I was eager to be involved.

'You can load out for me,' said my father.

'What does that mean?'

'Well, a bricklayer always needs a helper. Someone to make sure he has everything he needs close by. Loading out means you have to stack the bricks where I can reach them.'

It was agreed that I would be in charge not only of loading out, but also of passing my father the bricks. I was very excited. I stood poised with a brick in my hands ready for his instruction.

'I haven't laid a brick for over eight years,' he said, biting his lip and turning his trowel over uncertainly in his hand.

'Don't worry about it, Don Luigi. It will be like riding a bicycle,' Salvatore said kindly.

'I haven't ridden a bicycle for over eight years either,' my father replied.

The new oven took shape very gradually. Papá laid each brick with deliberate care, tapping it level with the handle of his trowel and cleaning the excess mortar from underneath with a single, skilful swipe. He stood back after each course was laid. It was like watching an artist at work.

'There was a time when I would have had this built in a couple of days,' he said, rubbing his back.

By the sixth day the work was almost complete, but despite his careful calculations, my father was one brick short.

'I could go and ask a few more people,' said Salvatore.

'Don't worry about that now. I just want to get this finished today,' replied my father. 'I know where I can get one.'

He limped off and came back a few minutes later carrying a brick. We did not ask where it had come from, but it later transpired that he had removed it from our front step. Knowing that my mother would not be pleased, he had covered the gap with a flower pot – but a displaced flower pot was easy for my eagle-eyed mother to spot.

She came marching into the laundry room as Salvatore, my father and I were standing back admiring our finished masterpiece. It was indeed a thing of beauty.

'I hope you intend to replace that brick very promptly,' she said sternly.

My father laughed. 'I don't suppose I will have any choice, my dear,' he replied. 'Now, what do you think of our oven?'

My mother conceded that it was a beautiful structure and that he had done a fine job.

'I may not be as quick as I was, but I can still lay a brick or two,' he said, then sniffed, turned away and wiped his eyes with his hat.

I had hoped that we would be eating pizza that very evening, but it was explained to me that it would be at least ten days until the mortar was sufficiently dry for the fire to be lit, and even then we would have to be careful. We would start with small fires and heat the structure gently over several days to ensure it was fully hardened.

We set a date for the grand opening. It was to be two weeks from the following Friday, which was market day in Cremona. Salvatore would go to the market that day and purchase fresh mozzarella.

My father checked the oven daily. He rubbed his finger gently along the mortar joints, gauging how dry they were. He was nervous about removing the supporting profile, but a week after its completion he declared that it was sufficiently set.

'This will be the moment of truth,' he said. 'Let's see if it holds together.'

Salvatore and my father slid the profile out between them and when the new oven did not collapse, they both cheered.

The first time the oven was lit it billowed out clouds of acrid, dust-laden smoke which wafted through the cracks around the door and invaded our kitchen, which made my mother yell as she was working on somebody's wedding sheets. However, as the new flue warmed, the smoke was drawn up the chimney.

The laundry room had never been heated and within a few hours of the oven being lit the walls wept with slimy, greenish condensation, which settled into puddles on the floor. The smell of a century of steam, sweat, soap and starch which had infused the plaster oozed into the air. It took four days for the heat to burn off the last of the moisture.

On the day of the great pizza-oven inauguration Salvatore set off early to pick up the mozzarella. He returned with his purchase in an excited and emotional state.

I watched as he kneaded dough with his good hand, then flopped it over his claw hand and stretched it until it was almost paper-thin.

'It has to be so thin you can see a beautiful woman's smile through it,' he said, then he turned to my aunt, saying, 'Smile for me, Donna Mina. Let me see if it's thin enough.'

My aunt told him to behave himself. Salvatore laughed and winked at me.

'Ah, you're too skinny for me anyway, Donna Mina. But maybe after you've eaten a few pizzas you'll fatten up and I'll agree to marry you.'

My aunt just rolled her eyes.

That evening, we set out a table under Zia Mina's vines and invited the Pozzettis to eat with us. Rita and I ate so much pizza that we felt quite sick.

'There's a future in pizza,' repeated Salvatore. 'I know there's a future in pizza.'

I didn't see Rita very much outside school as she was always busy helping her mother, who had given birth to twins a year after Pozzetti's return and now was pregnant again. Looking back, I think my aunt felt a little sorry for Rita and suggested that she should come over more often and play. She could bring the perambulator, my aunt said, and park it in the shade. We would all take turns bouncing the babies.

That summer, my aunt's old peach trees groaned under the weight of fruit. Fallen peaches carpeted the ground around them. The glut attracted swarms of large, aggressive wasps. The ominous drone of their approach provoked great fear, but Rita and I knew the procedure for avoiding their stings. We had to stand very still and not aggravate them. By doing this, they would soon lose interest and fly away.

We placed a muslin net over the pram to protect the babies and set about making a classroom for our dolls. Rita had brought along her peg dollies, which her father had carved for her. We played a game where my rag dolly taught her class of peg dollies to sing their times-tables. The peg dollies struggled with their seven times-table, but my rag dolly was a patient and kind teacher.

Suddenly Rita shrieked, leaped to her feet and began running around the peach tree, beating her arm.

'I've been stung!' she squealed. 'I've been stung! A wasp! A wasp stung me!'

'Zia Mina! Zia Mina!' I screamed. 'Come quick! Rita's been stung!'

My aunt, who was well-versed in old remedies, knew that in the case of a wasp sting the best thing to do was to suck out the poison with her mouth and immediately apply something cold and metallic to the area to stop the inflammation. As she was in her kitchen when she heard my cry for help, she grabbed the first metallic thing which came to hand. It was an enormous meat-cleaver with a broad blade.

Rita was not familiar with the procedure of applying cold metal to a wasp sting. On seeing my aunt emerge from the house brandishing a huge knife, she presumed that Zia Mina was about to hack the sting from her arm, or worse, remove the whole limb.

She ran away so fast that she almost burst the gate from its hinges, flew across the road without checking for traffic and was finally found whimpering under a bench in her father's workshop. It took quite some time to convince her that no part of her was going to be amputated.

As my aunt had not been able to catch Rita in time to suck out the poison and apply the cold metal, Rita's little arm swelled to twice its normal size. She was taken to the pharmacy in Mazzolo where the pharmacist gave her medicine and advised that dressings should be soaked in vinegar. Rita spent the following days sitting forlornly outside her house with her arm bandaged. She would not come anywhere near Paradiso for fear of being stung again. She smelled of vinegar for weeks. I saw even less of her after that.

The incident with the wasp made me wary of the peach trees. Salvatore said the fruit should be picked as quickly as possible or we would be plagued with even more wasps. He filled five crates with windfalls and there was still more fruit on the branches. My aunt preserved what she could, but the scarcity of sugar and paraffin to seal the jars caused there to be a glut of fresh fruit. Peaches could not be kept for long without spoiling.

Salvatore had garnered the affections of many people in the village. He had proved himself as a great organiser and always seemed to know someone who could help in some way. He had managed to charm Maestra Asinelli into giving him an old blackboard, which had been lying discarded in a corner of the schoolyard since I could remember.

He brought it back to Paradiso, cleaned it up and presented it to my aunt.

'What do you think, Donna Mina?' he said. 'We could place this by the roadside to advertise your produce. That way we'll get the passing trade as well as the market trade.'

Zia Mina declared that she thought it was an excellent idea. As Salvatore could not write well with his left hand, he tasked me with creating an advertisement in my best handwriting. Maestra Asinelli had even given him white and yellow chalk sticks.

My writing was much admired, but Salvatore suggested that I should include illustrations to make the advertisement more eye-catching. Unfortunately the quality of my artistic efforts did not match the clarity of my handwriting. My peaches just looked like misshapen childish circles.

My father, who had a certain talent for drawing, offered to help. He drew a beautiful frame of peaches around my words.

They were fabulously rounded and expertly shaded in white and yellow.

We all stood back to admire the board. There seemed to be some joke between my father and Salvatore, who winked and smirked at each other.

'What do you make of those peaches, Salvatore?' asked my father.

'They're perfect. Full and fleshy, just as God intended,' he replied.

'Yes. Thank God for lovely plump, ripe peaches.'

When Zia Mina came outside to look at our efforts, she scolded them both. She said there was nothing wrong with my writing, but insisted that I should rub out the peaches immediately because they looked like ladies' bottoms. My father should be ashamed of himself, she said.

Salvatore mumbled an excuse and went back to the vegetable garden. My father said nothing. I did as Zia Mina requested.

At some point later that day the illustrations reappeared, only this time they were drawn even more voluptuously. The resemblance to ladies' bottoms was unmistakable. My aunt sold every peach she had.

CHAPTER 12

At the end of November 1947 I heard news that Amilcare Marchesini had caught pneumonia and died. I felt a deep sorrow in my heart for Gianfrancesco. I could not imagine how it would feel to lose my father.

His funeral cortège passed our house. I had seen many coffins leave Pozzetti's workshop before, always carried on the shoulders of men, or sometimes on a cart, but I had never seen a rich person's funeral before. Two black horses with plumed headdresses pulled a black and gold hearse, behind which Signora Marchesini, smothered in black veils, and Gianfrancesco, white-faced and solemn, trudged in silence. They were followed by two dozen farmworkers and Fiorella. Behind them walked a long procession of villagers and strangers.

My father would have joined them if he had been able to walk the distance and had not been occupied waiting for Amilcare Marchesini's arrival at the cemetery. My mother said she saw no reason to attend the funeral. Zia Mina shut herself away and hung a string of rosary beads on her door, muttering something about a curse.

I stood by the gate and watched them go by, but Gianfrancesco did not see me. He kept his gaze fixed straight ahead.

When my father returned from work he said that Signora Marchesini had been inconsolable and had fainted from crying. Even my mother had to admit that she felt sympathy for her.

Although I had only met Amilcare Marchesini once and our meeting had been brief, I had liked him very much and thought of him often. Something compelled me to go and pay my respects.

Pieve Santa Clara's cemetery was built over a plague pit, so burials below ground were forbidden. This was not a rule specific to our village. There were strict laws throughout Italy. The pollution of the ground and poisoning of the water by the decomposing dead had long been understood.

Instead, coffins were placed in a system of pigeon-holes in the walls, then sealed with a slab bearing the deceased's name. Some had brackets with little vases attached for flowers. The newer tombs displayed a photograph. It was an efficient and space-saving way of housing the departed; like apartment blocks for the dead, stacked six bodies high.

Amilcare Marchesini had not been laid to rest in an ordinary pigeon-hole tomb. In the very centre of the cemetery, within its own fenced garden, stood the Marchesini mausoleum. It was a monumental thing, built to look like a Greek temple, complete with Corinthian columns and an intricately carved tympanum. It was as grand on the inside as it was on the outside. The words *In Paradisum Deducant te Angeli* – May the Angels Lead You into Paradise – were carved into the floor, along with a representation of the family coat of arms.

'I like it in here,' I said to my father. 'It's like a small house. I'd rather be buried in here than in a pigeon-hole.'

'Don't think about that, my little one,' he replied.

The names of several generations of Marchesinis were inscribed on the back wall. To the left were the ossuaries and to the right the newer tombs belonging to Amilcare Marchesini and his father, Carlo.

'Amilcare Marchesini didn't like his father. He was infamous,' I said.

My father frowned. 'Where did you hear that?'

'Gianfrancesco told me when I went to Cascina Marchesini with Mamma.'

'Well, let's hope they've reconciled their differences now that they're resting here together,' said my father. 'We can't choose our families. We just have to do our best to get on.'

'Why doesn't Zia Mina like the Marchesinis, Papá?'

'That's Zia Mina's business,' replied my father and ushered me out.

We sat together on the steps of the mausoleum with the sun on our faces.

'Do you get sad, working here?' I asked.

'Sometimes,' my father said. He pondered for a moment. 'I get sad when the people who come here are sad, when they've just lost somebody they love. But then gradually I see them come to terms with their loss and they're not so sad. Death is a part of life, my little one. It comes to all of us eventually. We just have to pray that it doesn't come too soon, when we still have things to do in our lives.'

'Like Amilcare Marchesini?'

'Yes. Just like Amilcare Marchesini.'

'And Ernesto.'

My father sighed. 'Yes,' he said quietly. 'Even more so for him.'

I had often been to Ernesto's tomb with my aunt, who visited it almost every time she went to the village, and always after church on Sunday. The epitaph read: *Ernesto Ponti, died 22nd October 1944, aged 12. Beloved son. Rest with the angels.*

'Ernesto would have been sixteen years old now. Almost a man,' said my father.

'Do you think he would still have been naughty?'

'I'm certain he would always have been spirited,' my father replied with a smile, then added, 'Do you want to meet my little friends?'

'Who are your friends?' I looked around.

'Watch this,' he said, and made a noise which was somewhere between a kiss and a whistle, then took a crust of bread from his pocket and ground it between his fingers. Within an instant a dozen sparrows had flown down and gathered at his feet.

'Hold out your hand very slowly,' he whispered. 'And don't make any noise.' He sprinkled crumbs into my palm. 'Now keep still and wait.'

One by one the sparrows hopped onto my hand to feed. The sharp taps of their tiny beaks tickled my palm. As soon as the bread was finished, they flew off.

'They share my lunch every day,' said my father. 'And now you've met my friends, you should come and meet the family.'

I helped my father to his feet. We walked slowly along the length of one wall, hand-in-hand, reading names and epitaphs. The sun reflected off the tall walls of tombs and scattered dappled patches along the gravel paths ahead of us. After a while my father stopped and pointed to a tomb on the third storey.

'That's my mother, your grandmother. Your grandfather is next to her. My aunt is just below them. And my uncle is just across there, right beside my cousin and his wife. And close by is Ernesto's father, my dear brother, Augusto.'

My father rubbed his back, took a sip of his medicine and said, 'I could tell you something about almost everybody here. That's the wonderful thing about being born in a little village like ours. Everybody knows everybody and there are so many stories. Sometimes I think about writing them all down, although I wouldn't know where to start.'

'You could start with you,' I suggested.

'I'm not dead yet,' he said. 'But I suppose I could. Maybe when you're older I'll tell you all the stories and you can write them down.'

I looked up and down the length of the wall. 'It would be a very long book.'

My father smiled and took another sip of medicine, joking, 'Well, my little one, at least if I go to heaven I won't be short of company.'

At the far end of the cemetery was a little rose garden with small stone and marble plaques and the occasional stubby cross set into the ground.

'This is the Garden of Little Angels,' explained my father. 'This part is for the little children who were taken too soon. Only babies can be buried in the ground here because their graves are shallow.' He pointed to a row of small grey plaques and said, 'Here, see if you can read these.'

I read out: 'Odetta Ponti, 1927; Oreste Ponti, 1928; Saverio Ponti, 1932; Marta Ponti, 1933.'

'They were your cousins. Ernesto's brothers and sisters.'

It took me a few moments to process what he said. It was too much to take in.

'All Ernesto's brothers and sisters died?'

'Yes.'

'But why did they die?'

'Life was hard then, my girl. Much harder than it is now. Lots of babies died if they were a little bit weak.'

I stood staring at the graves of my tiny dead cousins until my father squeezed my hand and led me further through the garden. Several rows behind my cousins was a much older grave, marked with a rusted metal cross.

'My own sister is buried here,' said my father.

'I didn't know you had a sister, Papá. Why did she die too?'

'She was born lifeless,' he said quietly. 'And when she went to heaven, she took our mother with her.'

'That's so sad.'

'It wasn't unusual then. I'm lucky to be alive myself. I was born too early and my mother couldn't make milk to feed me, so Pozzetti's mother wet-nursed me. That's why Pozzetti and I grew up like brothers. We are brothers in a way, milk brothers.'

I put my arms around my father and rested my head against him. He stroked my hair and placed his hand on my cheek.

'I'm glad you survived,' I said.

165

'I did. But only just. My sister's grave was meant for me.'

*

There had been a noticeable decline in the number of worshippers in church. Don Ambrogio had found himself entirely alone some week-day evenings and had been obliged to send the sacristan home and cancel Mass. Even the main Sunday service attendance was shrinking.

'Don Ambrogio's in quite a state about it,' my father told me one day. 'The tally for the collections is right down. The belfry's leaking and the front steps are subsiding. And the bullet damage has never been repaired properly. I'd offer to do it myself, but I don't think I could. Don Ambrogio has no idea how he's going to pay for it all. He's asked for more funds from the diocese, but everybody's in the same position. The bishop said there isn't enough money coming in.'

'It's all very well Don Ambrogio bellyaching about a diminished congregation,' Salvatore piped up, stroking his clawed hand, 'but I don't see him doing much to rouse his flock. His sermons send me to sleep. By the end, nobody's listening – that's if they were paying attention at all in the first place.'

'You're not wrong.' My father nodded in agreement.

'The thing is,' Salvatore continued, 'the law doesn't oblige anybody to go to church. People have to want to go of their own free will. People didn't come to my restaurant just because they were hungry. They came because they knew they were going to have not only good food, but a good time too. It's the same principle for the church. People want a sense of community, to be uplifted. All they're getting now is a boring sermon and then whining about money for repairs. Don Ambrogio has to understand that the more people enjoy themselves, the more willing they are to spend.'

'I don't know how Don Ambrogio would feel having his church compared with a restaurant,' my father grinned.

Salvatore shrugged. 'Nourishment of the body and nourishment of the spirit are not that dissimilar.'

'What would you suggest then?'

'Something to bring the community together, like a festival.'

'We do have the yearly procession for Santa Clara,' said my father.

'Oh yes. I forgot about the procession. And so did most of the village last year! The turn-out can't have been more than thirty and the average age must have been sixty. Young people don't want to follow a statue twice round the piazza.'

'I suppose not.' My father took a sip of his medicine.

'In Naples in the summer you can't move for festivals. Pieve Santa Clara could do with some entertainment. There should be a fête, a market and there should be good food and a dance in the evening. And fireworks too. Something to bring the community together and something which appeals to all the generations. And it's the fun and sense of community which should be the main focus. Not just handing out the begging bowl for the church repairs.'

Within half an hour Salvatore had set off to find Don Ambrogio.

The following Sunday Don Ambrogio announced that a day of festivities was to be held at the end of May. During the day there would be a fête with stalls and games and a football tournament open to teams, not only from Pieve Santa Clara, but from all the surrounding parishes. This would be followed by an open-air feast in the evening where entertainment would be provided by a band. The fact that it had been Salvatore's idea was not mentioned.

It was the talk of the village during the weeks which led up to it. Posters appeared in windows and on noticeboards advertising the great day and declaring that everybody was welcome.

167

Don Ambrogio could be seen bustling from house to house drumming up support. He seemed to be everywhere. Even those who tried their best to avoid him couldn't help but run into him. He arrived at Paradiso early one evening with a large notebook tucked under his arm and greeted my aunt rather more warmly than usual.

'Good evening, Signora Mina. It is a fine evening, is it not? May I say how splendid your vegetable garden is looking this year.'

My aunt nodded and replied, 'It hasn't been the best spring. We could have done with more rain.'

Don Ambrogio seated himself at her table under the vines and opened his notebook.

'As you are aware, being regular and diligent in your attendance at Mass, I am organising a most marvellous day in an attempt to unify and reconvene some members of our precious congregation.'

'Of course I'm aware,' replied my aunt. 'It was Salvatore's idea.'

'Indeed,' said Don Ambrogio, then licked his index finger and turned to the appropriate page in his book. 'It will not surprise you therefore that I am here in my capacity as a most humble servant of the church to request a pledge towards our special day. Firstly, could I ask whether you will be reserving a place for a stall?'

'A stall?'

'The first part of the day will be given over to a fête to be held in the garden beside the church, and if more space is required due to the high demand, space will be made in the piazza.'

'What sort of a stall do you have in mind?'

'The choice would be entirely yours, Signora Mina. Perhaps a game involving fishing for prizes? Or a lucky dip? Both could be very popular.'

My aunt frowned. 'I think there are others better placed to organise that type of thing,' she said briskly.

'Very well,' replied Don Ambrogio, turning to another page.

'If not a stall for games, perhaps one from which to sell your fine produce?'

'I already sell my produce at the markets in Pieve Santa Clara and in Mazzolo.'

'But this would be different, Signora Mina. This would be for the benefit of the parish. As you are aware, we are using this event to raise money for some much-needed repairs to the church. Unfortunately, everybody insists on being paid for their work nowadays. It's a sad reflection of the material times in which we live.'

Don Ambrogio sighed and looked wistfully into the distance, then turned back to my aunt.

'We are asking that each stallholder contributes 1,000 lire for their pitch and fifty per cent of their proceeds from the sales.'

My aunt raised her eyebrows and coughed.

'A thousand lire and fifty per cent on top!' she exclaimed. 'I'm not sure about that.'

'Very well,' replied Don Ambrogio. 'I quite understand that you might need time to think about it. I'll put you down as a maybe.'

My aunt crossed her arms and frowned as Don Ambrogio wrote in his notebook.

'However, Signora Mina, I would recommend that you don't spend too long thinking about it as spaces are limited.'

'How many pitches have been reserved?'

Don Ambrogio leafed back through his book and ran his finger down a long list.

'Three definites. Twenty-two possibles at present. But things can change very, very quickly, so I would encourage you to think about it this evening and supply your answer tomorrow. I would hate for you to be disappointed.'

The priest took a handkerchief from somewhere in the folds of his cassock and ran it across his forehead.

'The second matter for which I need your consideration is that of the feast which is to be held in the evening following the fête and the football tournament. It will be quite an occasion, Signora Mina! We expect capacity attendance and are looking forward to not only our stomachs being satiated, but also our ears entertained by a local band of excellent reputation whose musical services have been enjoyed as far afield as Mantova and Piacenza.'

My aunt said that sounded very nice, but she wasn't really very interested in hearing a band.

'I fully understand, Signora Mina. I expect your musical tastes to lean more towards the Arcadian folk era of our childhoods. But unfortunately, the younger generation do not care too much for our wonderful old *canti popolari*. And it is the younger generation in particular whom we are hoping to encourage back into the fold.'

Don Ambrogio then proceeded to hum something which may well have been intended as a rendition of a *canto popolare*, but sounded more like a wasp trapped in a bottle.

'Apologies, Signora Mina. I digress! Allow me to move onto the matter of the feast.' Don Ambrogio took a very deep breath, licked his lips and spread his hands flat on the table, as though already envisaging a banquet laid out before him.

'Amongst the delicacies which we propose will be spit-roasted pig, a wide variety of grilled meats, polenta, bread and soup. Our intention is to charge diners a fee of 200 lire per head, payable in advance. This will not include wine, of course. That will be available to be bought separately on the night.'

Don Ambrogio looked at my aunt as though he was expecting something.

'Are you asking me to pay you now?' she said.

'Indeed, Signora Mina. Although we are receiving pledges and donations of food, a good part of it will have to be purchased before the event. Regrettably, I am not in the same position as

Our Lord and Saviour Jesus Christ, Who was able to perform miracles with loaves and fishes. Nor do I have the ability to turn water into wine.'

Don Ambrogio chuckled, although it was clear that the joke had been told many times before, probably to every household he had visited on his rounds.

My aunt thought about this for a few moments and promised a crate of spring cabbages for the soup. Don Ambrogio hesitated before writing down her pledge.

'Cabbages?' he mused. 'Although that is most generous, I already have several promises of cabbage.'

'That's because they're in season,' replied my aunt.

'Indeed,' said Don Ambrogio. 'In that case we will all be enjoying a hearty cabbage soup. And please don't think me in any way ungrateful for your generosity. Many people are very fond of cabbage soup. Adding a few rashers of *pancetta* would of course add to its tastiness.'

'Are you expecting me to donate *pancetta*?' asked my aunt.

'Thank you, Signora Mina. That would be marvellous! You are most generous.'

My aunt said that she would see what she could do, adding after Don Ambrogio had left that pledging a crate of cabbages was one thing, but *pancetta* did not grow in her garden. She was surprised that he hadn't requested that she play in one of the football teams, or join the band.

*

Piles of old newspapers were delivered to school, and our classes were suspended for a whole day so that we could make bunting. Maestra Asinelli organised us in a strict production line. I was put in charge of cutting. Rita was my second-in-command.

We worked through our lunchtime and two hours past the end

171

of the school day. Our enormous lengths of bunting were strung between the houses in the village and across the front of every shop. Even the church was festooned. Despite its lack of colour, the bunting was a very pretty sight as it fluttered in the breeze.

The village was abuzz. Pavements and roads were swept, doorsteps scrubbed, the little garden beside the church was raked and its shrubs trimmed. All rubbish was removed. The whole village gleamed.

Much attention was paid to preparation of the football pitch. However, there was a certain level of disgruntlement amongst the teams when they came to inspect the grounds. Pieve Santa Clara's football pitch was situated on a piece of land which sloped – something that was both unusual and unfortunate in an area as flat as Pieve Santa Clara. There was also a problem with the goals. One had rotted beyond repair and the replacement which had been procured was considerably smaller.

Following much arguing it was decided that in order to make things fairer, the best option was to place the large goal at the top of the slope and the small goal at the bottom.

It was not a solution which pleased everybody. It certainly did not please Pierino Gambetta, who was Mazzolo's star player and something of a local celebrity. His fame arose from the fact that he had almost been selected to play in Cremona's reserve football team – twice.

The size of the goals and the camber of the pitch were not the only causes of disagreement. The idea had been for teams from local parishes to participate, but when a team comprising members of the regional Communist Party put its name forward, there was some questioning as to whether this was appropriate.

Not wishing to discriminate and seeing this as a great opportunity to bring the disenfranchised back under the wing of the church, Don Ambrogio approved the registration. This led Pieve Santa Clara's Christian Democrat mayor to complain that if the Communists could enrol a team, other political parties could do so too. A Christian Democrat team was scrambled together very quickly. The centre-forward and the right back were actually supporters of the Liberal Party, and the goalkeeper was a paid-up member of the Radicals, but nobody opposed the coalition.

On the Sunday preceding the auspicious day, Don Ambrogio announced that the fête was to be an occasion which would be remembered by all for years to come. And the way things turned out, he was proved to be absolutely right.

*

As the great day approached, the weather seemed uncertain. Warm May sunshine could usually be relied upon, but instead a cold front came in from the north-east, bringing with it a colossal amount of rain. The day before the fête, a week's worth of spring rain fell in two hours, washing the newspaper bunting into a gluey, grey pulp, which stuck to the streets and clogged the drains, causing some cellars in the village to flood.

The football pitch, which suffered from poor drainage at the best of times, became waterlogged. Questions were asked as to whether the event would still be going ahead and Don Ambrogio insisted that it must.

'People have made arrangements at considerable personal inconvenience and even taken time off work!' he exclaimed. 'We cannot possibly change the day. And quite apart from that, all the food which has been pledged and prepared would spoil. The day must and will go ahead as planned.'

I went down to the village early in the morning with Rita. Our mothers had given us 20 lire each and we were eager to spend it at the stalls. But when we arrived we found only four stalls. One sold nougat at double the usual price, probably in order to cover the commission required. The second would have sold roasted pine nuts if the charcoal had not been too damp to burn. The last two were run by children who had been given free pitches as there had not been enough takers. There was a stall where upon payment of 50 lire players could throw hoops over bottles, and one where for the same payment balls could be thrown at skittles. Unfortunately there were very few keen to play either game as there were no prizes involved. Rita and I couldn't afford to play even if we had wanted to.

Despite the disappointing fête, everybody was looking forward to the afternoon's football tournament, but as the hour of the first kick-off approached, the heavens opened again and released an enormous deluge which fell so heavily that it was painful on the skin. One man remarked that it was enough to drown the birds in the trees.

Each match was to last only forty minutes to allow all the teams to play and a champion to be crowned by six o'clock, but there was so much stoppage time due to slips and falls and disagreements that the first game took well over an hour. The second match was worse as the pitch was by now such a mud-bath that most of the time it was difficult to see the ball. Passing it between players became impossible as it kept getting stuck in the mire. Pierino Gambetta, Mazzolo's star player, walked off saying that it was beneath him to play in such conditions. The crowd booed and threw clods of earth at him.

By the third game the players were so caked in mud that it was difficult to tell who was playing for which team. Not even the players could tell. Four own-goals were scored.

In the crowd we grew colder and colder and when it started to rain again most people went home. The teams decided to call the tournament off. Even the Communists, Christian Democrats, Liberals and the Radical agreed unanimously.

Still, despite the disappointment of the abandoned tournament, there was a feast to look forward to and it was agreed that a bellyful of hot, nourishing food was just what everybody needed.

'Nothing can be done about the weather. It's pointless getting cross about it,' said my father.

However, the mayor refused to have the municipal tables and chairs put outside for fear they would be damaged by the rain. Instead, people were advised to bring umbrellas and not to forget their hats.

There was much grumbling.

'How's a man supposed to eat his grub if he's holding his plate in one hand and an umbrella in the other?' said one.

'Don Ambrogio should open up the church and we can eat our dinner in there,' suggested another.

This was deemed to be a good idea by some, but not by Don Ambrogio, who refused point blank.

'Why?' came several cries. 'Why can we not sit in the pews?'

'Because the House of God is not the place to eat one's dinner! It is against the teachings,' Don Ambrogio said firmly.

'What teachings? You're just making things up!'

He protested that he most certainly was not – and denied that he had once been seen tucking into a *panino* behind the pulpit.

'It says so very clearly in Corinthians,' he blustered. 'And anyway, the mess you would all leave would be an unholy one. I wouldn't put it past you to rinse your greasy fingers in the stoup. It's totally out of the question.'

The band turned up, but refused to play unless their fee was paid upfront, so they left.

Tempers were becoming frayed. People were cold and their stomachs were empty. The bad situation was made worse by the fact that when at last the promised feast materialised, it was not much of a feast at all.

A very small piglet had been roasted. My father commented that had it not been for its snout and curly tail it could have been mistaken for a cat. The selection of meats comprised half a dozen skinny sausages and chops which were more bone than meat.

The huge cauldron of polenta was cold and barely a third full. The soup was thin and leafy and, despite my aunt's donation, contained no *pancetta*. There were complaints that the bread was stale. Some loaves bore the nibble-marks of rats.

As for the wine, there was plenty of it, but everybody complained about the extortionate price being charged for a very small glass.

People were angry and demanded their money back. In order to placate the crowd Don Ambrogio conceded that they could have the wine for free.

I cannot be certain at what point the general disgruntlement descended into a drunken brawl, but before long the piazza was the scene of a great thrashing of fists and shouts of blasphemous swearing. Stones were thrown. Sticks whistled through the air, bruising backs and cracking skulls. Several shop windows were broken.

It became so bad that the police were called, but being seriously outnumbered by the rabble, they barricaded themselves into the hairdresser's, where they remained until the crowd had cudgelled itself to exhaustion and headed home.

*

It was a subdued Don Ambrogio who welcomed his flock the following Sunday.

Barely a third of the pews were filled as many parishioners were unable to attend owing to the injuries they had sustained in the brawl. Others were at home in bed with heavy colds and rheumatic aches caused by standing outside in soaked clothing.

Don Ambrogio delivered a long and tedious sermon on the authority of God's Word and directed everybody's attention to the collection tin. The festival was not mentioned.

CHAPTER 13

My final year of elementary school was a happy one. I learned well and looked forward to each day, but I was saddened by the fact that once I moved up to middle school, Maestra Asinelli would no longer be my teacher.

We were all so keen to please her that many of us brought her fruit or flowers almost every day. Finally she had to request that we did not bring so many gifts or she would have no space to work. Her desk looked like a still-life composition.

'You are all such kind children and I am very grateful for everything you bring, but rather than having all these gifts accumulating on my desk, I am going to propose an idea to you. On Sunday, after church, we will set up a little stall in the piazza. We will sell this fruit and anything else you might wish to bring in. I propose that with the money raised, if it is enough, we will go on a school outing at the end of the year to celebrate our time together. I will miss you all so much when you move up to middle school. What do you all think about that?'

There was much excitement. Suggestions were made as to suitable destinations for our trip, ranging from Rome to Paris. Maestra Asinelli said that if enough money was raised for a trip to Rome or Paris, that is where we would go, but we should not be disappointed if we had to limit our travel ambitions to somewhere considerably closer.

As it turned out, there was not enough money for a trip to Rome or Paris, but we did take the train to Cremona. I had been on the train once before, but had been too young to remember.

I sat transfixed, looking out of the window as fields of crops and cows, little houses, farms and barns flashed past. As we approached Cremona, the houses bunched together in clusters until finally I could see nothing but houses, buildings and people. Everybody seemed to be very busy.

Maestra Asinelli took us to visit the Cathedral of Santa Maria Assunta, which she told us had taken nearly four hundred years to build. We climbed on the backs of the great stone lions which flanked its entrance and ate our packed lunches sitting on the steps.

She told us that Cremona was world-famous for its violin factory and how a man called Antonio Stradivari had made the best violins in the world there. It was also famous for its *torrone*, the most delicious nougat made with honey and almonds. We had little interest in violins, but we all knew about *torrone*. For most of us it was the best thing about Christmas.

I am certain that our day in Cremona was every bit as exciting and educational as a trip to Paris or Rome would have been.

My contribution to the stall which had funded our excursion had been two purses I had made out of handkerchiefs. I had attached a ribbon to each so that they could be worn around the neck. Maestra Asinelli complimented me on my skill and told me that I would make an excellent seamstress, like my mother. However, I had other ideas.

As class was dismissed, I lingered behind.

'Aren't you going home, Graziella?' asked Maestra Asinelli. She was at her desk correcting our exercise books.

'I wanted to ask you a question.'

'Of course. Ask me anything you want.'

'How do you become a teacher?'

Maestra Asinelli smiled. 'Is that what you would like to do?'

'Yes. I think so.'

'Well, once you have completed middle school you will have to go to the Istituto Magistrale. It's a school for teachers. If you pass your exams you will be able to teach in an elementary school, like me.'

'Are the exams hard?'

Maestra Asinelli rested her chin on her hand and thought before she replied.

'They require diligence,' she told me, 'but I am certain they would not be beyond your capabilities. In fact, I think you would make an excellent teacher, Graziella.'

I flushed with pride. 'Do you think so?'

'I *know* so. Teaching is an excellent vocation. The fact you are thinking of it as a career whilst so young shows you have great maturity.'

I was not sure what a vocation or a career was, but I knew that maturity was a good thing.

'Did you always want to be a teacher, Maestra Asinelli?'

'Yes. Since I was about your age. And I did exactly what you have just done. I stayed behind after class and asked my teacher what I should do so that I could be a teacher too. And I'm very glad that I did. I cannot think that I will ever want to do anything else.'

The end of term saddened me greatly. I knew I would miss Maestra Asinelli very much, but I passed my elementary exam with ease and secured my place at the middle school in Mazzolo the following autumn.

*

It was the afternoon of 26 June 1949. I was in my aunt's vegetable garden helping to harvest peas. June was always a beautiful month, when the temperature was not too high and the days were long. Insects hummed and birdsong was a constant accompaniment to our work. There were so many butterflies that we regarded them as pests. They would fly into our faces and tangle in our hair.

We finished picking the pods and took our basket from the garden to the vine-covered veranda by the kitchen door where we sat side by side on the doorstep. The cat came to sit with us and arranged itself by Zia Mina's feet.

My aunt wedged her metal bowl between her knees and we set to work, popping the hard peas out of their pods and into the bowl.

'I think I would like to be a teacher, like Maestra Asinelli,' I said.

My aunt nodded her approval, then added, 'You will have to study hard.'

'I will have to go to the Istituto Magistrale and take teaching exams.'

'You are very well informed,' my aunt said. She seemed impressed.

'What did you want to be when you were little, Zia Mina?'

She shrugged. 'It wasn't the same when I was a child. I was sent out to work in the rice fields. That was the only choice I had.'

'How old were you?'

'Barely ten years old. By your age I'd already been working two years.' Her face darkened. 'It was horrible work. No better than slave labour.'

I already knew that Zia Mina had worked in the rice fields in her youth. I knew it because she complained about it frequently. If ever anybody grumbled about hard work, or an aching back, or miserly pay, Zia Mina would lecture them about the hardship the rice workers endured.

The only picture my aunt possessed of herself as a young woman was taken whilst she was working in the rice fields. It was a group photograph of a dozen girls wearing wide-brimmed hats and handkerchiefs over their faces as protection from the blazing sun and insect bites.

In the photograph my aunt was only recognisable as she was the tallest amongst the young women, but years of bending double in the rice fields had affected her posture. She stood slightly stooped with her neck arched forwards. Her long, bony legs and broad hips had afforded her the nickname 'The Heron' amongst the rice workers. She had never cared for it much.

We sat chatting, the sound of hard, fresh peas pinging off the sides of the bowl. I stole the occasional one when my aunt wasn't looking. Her cat lay sunning its belly in a patch of sunshine which pierced through the vines.

Suddenly we were interrupted by the sound of the garden gate flying open and a young boy racing up the path towards us, scattering the gravel with his hasty steps. I knew him from church. He was an altar boy.

'Where's Signora Ponti?' he called, breathless.

My aunt looked up and asked, 'Which one?'

'Luigi Ponti's wife!'

'In her house, working. What is it?'

'It's Signor Ponti. There's been an accident!'

My aunt swiftly set the bowl aside, glanced down at me and told me to stay where I was. Then she ran into the house with the boy and moments later, emerged with my mother.

'Wait there, Graziella,' called my mother and I watched as the three of them darted away, through the gate and off down the road.

I sat on the step, trying to make sense of what had happened. I didn't know whether I was more sad or scared. Another accident would mean more pain for my father. Worse still, it would mean he could no longer work, even for Don Ambrogio. What would we do then?

I tried to distract myself by shelling the remaining peas and confiding my fears to the cat. It rolled onto its back and purred loudly.

It felt like an eternity before Rita's mother was sent to find me. Her expression was solemn.

'Graziella,' she said softly, kneeling down with some effort due to her bulging, pregnant belly. 'Your Papá has been taken to hospital. He had a fall.'

Fear rose through me in a sickening wave.

'Has Mamma gone with him?'

'Yes, she has. So has your aunt. I want you to come with me until they get home.' She reached out her hand and took mine.

'Will he be all right?' I asked.

'Only the doctors will know that. So just stay with me until we receive news – and try not to worry too much.'

Rita was not there. She had gone to help her grandmother, so I sat quietly, trying to play with her dolls' house. I had long been envious of Rita's dolls' house, which her father had made for her out of a vegetable crate. I had never had it to myself before, but I found it impossible to invent a game which comforted me.

After some time, Pozzetti returned, smiled and squeezed my cheek, but there was a troubled look on his face. He had a whispered conversation with his wife and went to his workshop.

Rita arrived home just before supper. Her presence alleviated my worry a little, but the lack of any news about my father made me a joyless playmate.

'What if he can't work any more?' I asked.

Rita clutched my hand and said, 'My father will help him. Just like he does when he takes him to work on the back of the bicycle. Papá says that friends always help each other.'

This was a little glimmer of comfort in the dark pit of my distress.

Rita's mother served a supper of pork and beans, but I couldn't eat, despite the fact that I was used to strict rules about eating what was placed in front of me without question or complaint, even if I didn't like it.

'Try to eat something, Graziella. You will feel better,' said Pozzetti. But I could not. I couldn't even swallow any of the vanilla custard Rita's mother had made to cheer me up.

After supper Rita and I helped to dry dishes and once the washing-up was complete, we took turns to wash ourselves in the sink. I was given Rita's spare nightdress and her mother combed and braided our hair.

'What an adventure for you to sleep together,' she said cheerfully. I was unsure about this as my bed-sharing memories in the convent were not fond ones.

As the church clock struck nine in the distance and we were preparing to say good night, my aunt appeared at the door. I knew by her swollen eyes that something terrible had happened. I stood paralysed – I do not know how long for – but by the time I regained my senses, everybody in the room was crying. I don't recall how I was told, or who told me, but I knew.

My father was dead.

He had fallen from a ladder, two floors up. Don Ambrogio had asked him to deal with a wasps' nest under the eaves of his residence. My father had lost his footing, probably due to a back spasm, and had fallen. By the time he reached hospital, there was nothing they could do for him.

The grief which overwhelmed me made me sick. I cried and shook in my aunt's arms until I was limp and drained of all feeling.

Pozzetti carried me home, where my mother was sitting white-faced and red-eyed at the kitchen table. She was barely able to speak, save to curse Don Ambrogio for asking a man in my father's condition to do something so risky; and my father for accepting.

Over the days that followed, people came and went from our house to pay their respects. Once they had been to see us, they moved on to Rita's. I assumed that they were going there because her father and mine had been so close. It was only when I overheard a snippet of conversation between my aunt and someone who had come to offer his condolences, that I realised that my father was laid out at Pozzetti's. Our kind neighbour was, after all, the undertaker.

'Zia Mina, is Papá at Pozzetti's?' I asked.

My aunt bent down, ruffled my hair and said, 'Yes.'

'Have all those people been going to see him?'

'Yes.'

'Can I go too?'

My aunt paused for a moment. 'Is that what you want?'

'Yes.'

'Let me talk to your Mamma,' she said.

I wanted to see my father more than I could express. My aunt told me to be patient, and three days after the accident, which was the day before the funeral, my request was granted.

Zia Mina walked me across the road to Pozzetti's where my father was laid out in a room next to the workshop. It was a room which was always locked and out of bounds. Even Rita had only been allowed in there once, and only because there was, quite literally, *no body* in there.

The room was nothing like Pozzetti's sawdust-strewn workshop. It was immaculate, with a tiled floor and a large, clean workbench. Empty coffins stood propped upright against the wall. My father's coffin was resting on a stand, which was too high to allow me a proper view of him. Pozzetti lifted me into his arms so I could see.

The coffin was lined with a white sheet. My father's head rested on a pillow which had been embroidered by my mother as a gift for Rita's parents. Had I not known he was dead, I would have thought him asleep – apart from the fact that he was lying on his back, something his injuries would never have allowed him to do whilst alive. His skin was pale, but smooth and free from the familiar lines of pain etched into his expression. His hair had been brushed carefully and his hands had been placed together in a position of prayer against his chest. He was wearing his best suit, which was too big for him as it had been purchased years before, for his wedding. His frame had shrunk significantly since then. My mother regretted having had neither the time nor the spirit to alter it.

Pozzetti held me for a long time, letting me take in the final image of my father. His stubbly cheek prickled against mine. He smelled of sawdust.

'Is there anything you would like to put in the coffin before I close it?' he asked. 'Something you would like your Papá to take to heaven with him?'

'What will he need in heaven?'

'Something to remind him of you.'

I darted back to Paradiso, took my special handkerchief embroidered with cherries and blossom and ran back to Pozzetti.

'Did you make this?' he asked. I nodded.

'What a beautiful thing! Let's put it on his chest. That way, you will always be close to his heart.'

He lifted me with one arm and together we placed the handkerchief, folded into a triangle, into the breast pocket of my father's suit.

'Can I touch him?' I asked.

'If you want.'

I brushed my fingertips against my father's, then traced them across his cold cheek, before craning my neck and placing the gentlest of kisses on his forehead.

'Will Papá's back still hurt in heaven?'

'No. Nobody feels any pain in heaven.'

'Ernesto will be happy to see him,' I said, 'and his Mamma and his Papá. He knows a lot of dead people. He's going to be very busy. Do you think he'll have time to watch over me?'

Pozzetti nodded and held me a little tighter.

'Of course,' he replied. 'He'll always be watching over you and your Mamma because you were the most important people in his life.'

I didn't cry. I felt an extraordinary, almost euphoric, sense of peace; and for as long as I live I will be thankful to Rita's kind and caring father for his compassion and for allowing my final farewell to my father to have been so full of love.

*

Pozzetti made a coffin from wood which my mother could never have afforded. The lid did not match the sides, but nobody paid attention to such a trivial detail. It had ornate brass handles, one of which did not match either, but nobody mentioned it. This was Pozzetti's parting gift for my father, his milk brother and lifelong friend.

My mother had not wanted Don Ambrogio, whom she considered responsible for my father's death, to conduct the funeral service. She refused to see him when he called at the house to say that the parish would provide a tomb free of charge in recognition of Papá's services. Don Gervaso, the thin, quiet priest whose charitable organisation had employed my father was brought in instead.

I have only a hazy recollection of the funeral. There was no cortège and no hearse. My father's coffin was carried to the church by Pozzetti, Salvatore and four other men. I felt lost and small in the mass of black-clad mourners. I held my aunt's hand. Rita's mother read a prayer. My mother sobbed.

Over the next few weeks, I was kept busy by my aunt. I was given sole use of the bedroom as my mother elected to take over my father's old bed in the corner of the kitchen.

I felt a deep yearning for my Papá. Bedtime was the worst time, when I felt it most. I missed drifting off to sleep to the sound of my parents talking in the kitchen. I missed their exchange of news, my father's chuckle, his anecdotes and stories. Sometimes Zia Mina would come and sit with my mother and they would talk for a while, but it was not the same. Their conversations were domestic and mundane. I missed my father's conversations with my mother as much as I missed his conversations with me.

Papá's jacket and trousers hung on a hook on the kitchen wall for a long time after his death. Sometimes I would press my cheek to the fabric, close my eyes and breathe in, imagining for a few moments that he was still inside the garments. Perhaps my mother did the same, although I never saw her do it.

I think that for my mother, my father's death was a horrible relief.

CHAPTER 14

In September 1949, less than three months after my father's death, I began middle school. A brand new school building had been constructed in Mazzolo to take children from Mazzolo, Pieve Santa Clara and other adjoining villages.

The building was enormous compared with the old schoolhouse I had been used to. It had high-ceilinged classrooms with large windows, and gargantuan cast-iron radiators. The air always smelled of disinfectant.

We no longer had wooden desks with inkwells, inscribed with a century's worth of graffiti from previous pupils' schooldays, but smart, newly-designed models with chrome legs and green plastic tops. Everything was fresh and modern. There were murals made out of tiles down the walls of each corridor and metal lockers in which to store our belongings. There was even a sports hall.

It was a noisy, intimidating place, full of children I did not know who were so much bigger than me. I had counted upon having Rita for support in class. However, there were two classes in each year, and Rita and I were both dismayed to find that we were not in the same class. We saw each other at break-time in the yard and during our journey to and from school, but I missed having her beside me.

The corridors echoed with the commotion of children bustling their way from class to class, shouting for their classmates. I cannot count how many times I was hit by carelessly swinging satchels, or walked into by schoolchildren too busily engaged in conversation to notice a very small girl like me.

A school bus would stop to pick us up outside my house every morning at half past seven and deliver us back outside Rita's when the school day was finished.

I no longer had a single form teacher, but different teachers for different subjects, which I found confusing. I missed Maestra Asinelli. I seemed to have lost my way and also my concentration, whether I was reading, writing, attempting to learn mathematics or the new subjects which now filled my timetable. I knew little about history, geography or natural sciences, and even less about Latin. The Latin prayers I had memorised in church and at the convent were of no use. I studied aimlessly in the hope that something I read or copied out might lodge itself somewhere in my brain, but very little did.

My father's death was still so close that no matter what I was trying to do, however interesting or involved, he would float into my mind and occupy the space. There seemed to be no room for anything else. Each time I thought of him I felt tears well in my eyes. I would wipe them on my cuff hoping nobody had noticed. Nobody did.

The grief I suffered was compounded by a new anxiety. I was terrified that I might also lose my mother. I would torture myself with visions that she too could have an accident, or become afflicted with some incurable illness. My father had lost both his parents very young. My mother had lost hers before I was born. Zia Mina had been orphaned as a baby. The terror of being left both fatherless and motherless overwhelmed me. I felt it like a heaviness in my head.

On the third day of my second week I was given a detention for daydreaming and I missed the bus home. When I was finally allowed to leave, the school building was silent. A cleaner in a brown overall was mopping the corridors. I skirted around the edge of the wet floor and made my way to the front door. My mother was not going to be pleased.

'Graziella?' said a voice from behind me.

189

I turned around and saw a tall, tousle-haired boy with round, silver-rimmed spectacles. A heavy bag of books was slung across his body. It looked as though it was about to cut him in half diagonally.

'Do you remember me?'

It was Gianfrancesco Marchesini.

'Yes, of course I remember you! How are you?'

'Fine, thank you,' he said politely. 'How are you?'

'I'm fine too, thank you.'

'I heard about your father,' he went on. 'I'm very sorry for you. I lost my father too.'

'I know. I'm sorry for you too.'

As the words left my lips, I felt the sting of tears scald my eyes. My nose prickled. My mouth was instantly dry. As usual, I wiped my eyes on my cuff, hoping he hadn't seen, but when I looked up, his eyes were also shimmering.

'What are you doing here?' I asked, swallowing hard.

'This is where I go to school now,' he replied with an air of resignation.

'Why don't you go to school in Cremona any more?'

He shrugged, his heavy book bag cutting into his shoulder. 'Things are different now. My mother can't afford to pay the fees. They offered me a scholarship, but a scholarship doesn't cover the boarding fees or the extras.'

'What's a scholarship?'

'It's when a school offers to educate good students free of charge.' Gianfrancesco looked down at his satchel and sighed, 'But now I'm a whole year behind. I should be in the third year, but they've made me repeat the second year because I missed so much school after my father died.'

He pretended to straighten his glasses, although I could see that really he was wiping his eyes.

'Anyway,' he went on, 'it's better that I'm not away at school all week. It's hard for my mother being all alone in the house. At least now I can keep her company in the evenings.'

He gathered himself and took a deep breath.

'Why are you here so late?' he asked. 'Don't you have to catch the school bus?'

'Yes. But I got a detention.'

'That's too bad.'

'And you? Did you get a detention too?'

'No. I stayed behind to study because I wanted to.'

We walked together out of the school gates. His book bag was so full that he was forced to bend forwards to counter-balance the weight.

'How are you getting home?' he wanted to know. 'Are you catching the public bus? I'm planning to catch the next one.'

'I'm going to walk. I don't have any money.'

'I can pay for you. It's a very long way to walk with a full satchel.'

'I don't know when I can pay you back. I can't ask my mother for money, not when I missed the bus because of a detention.'

'Don't worry,' said Gianfrancesco. 'You don't have to pay me back.'

We had to wait forty minutes for the bus. Gianfrancesco bought a bag of toasted pumpkin seeds from a grocers' shop and we sat together, splitting the husks between our teeth.

'Do you like the new school?' I asked.

'I've done most of the work before, and far more thoroughly,' he replied flatly.

'Then you can be top of your class,' I chirped, but he seemed unconvinced.

'I suppose so. I think it will be better when I have some friends.'

'I'm your friend.'

Gianfrancesco smiled and said, 'Yes. In that case, things are better already.'

He tipped the last of the seeds into my hand, then screwed up the paper wrapper and slipped it into his satchel. I licked my fingertip and dipped it in the salt.

'Why don't you catch the school bus?' I asked. 'It goes right past the end of your driveway.'

'My mother said she would drop me off and pick me up in the car.'

'Oh. Why isn't she picking you up today then?'

He fiddled with the buckle on his bag. Then: 'I asked her not to. Some of the boys here were taunting me about it.'

'Why would they taunt you?'

'They don't like me because I was at a private school before.'

'That's ridiculous. Why should they be bothered about something like that?'

'Well, it seemed to concern them a great deal They pushed me into the wall and threw my books on the floor.'

'Did you tell?'

'I've told you.'

'How about your mother? Did you tell her?'

'No. I didn't want to worry her. I just asked her not to bring me by car any more. That's why I'm catching the public bus. It gives me a reason to stay behind and study anyway.'

Gianfrancesco adjusted his spectacles and continued, 'Those same boys got me into trouble before.'

'How?'

'You remember when that tobacco train was held up?'

'Yes.'

'Well, two of the farmhands wanted to go and get some tobacco and I went with them. I didn't tell my parents because I knew they would forbid it. I didn't go with the intention of taking any tobacco – I was just curious to see a derailed train. But one of the farmhands gave me a sack anyway and told me to fill it up, so I did. I thought that as there were so many people helping themselves, it wouldn't matter. Anyway, word spread that the police were coming and people scattered. I couldn't find the farmhands. I asked a group of boys if they had seen them and they told me they had gone towards Mazzolo. So I went in that direction, only to walk straight into a police blockade with a sack full of stolen tobacco on my back. They arrested me for theft and took me to the police station in Cremona in the back of a van. The boys who told me to go that way were the same ones who were taunting me the other day. They sent me towards Mazzolo on purpose because they knew the police were there.'

'That's terrible!' I was shocked. 'What did your parents say?'

'My father was angry and my mother was incandescent. I had to do some pretty disgusting chores for the rest of the summer holiday as punishment. When you came back to my house with your mother, I saw you. But I was cleaning out the slurry pit – I was in it up to my knees. I couldn't come and say hello when I was in that state.'

Finally, the bus drew up in the square where we were waiting and we got on. It was empty, but we sat at the back anyway. Ten minutes later we had pulled up by the old gateposts.

'Will you come to my house again?' Gianfrancesco asked.

'When?'

'On Saturday.'

'If my mother will let me.'

'Tell her we have a good crop of pears. You can have some to take home. As many as you want.'

When the bus stopped outside Paradiso a few minutes later, my mother was standing by the gate, her hands on her hips.

'Where on earth have you been? I was worried sick!'

My explanation did not please her and she huffed as I crossed the threshold.

Since my father's death my mother had hardened. She said that she refused to let grief incapacitate her, but she had become sterner and more insular. Her patience was easily tested and I did everything in my power not to irritate her, which was easier said than done because everything did seem to irritate her, apart from her embroidery work. She focused on it from the moment she got up in the morning until the light faded, and spoke very little. Conversation, even if it was about something pleasant, seemed to darken her dark moods further. Any questions I asked were either ignored or met with a brief answer, then she would shut down. She rarely mentioned my father.

My mother had always had a way of soothing me by telling me that things would be all right. It was that assurance which had helped me through my long months of exile at the convent. Sometimes I thought she said it not just to convince me, but to convince herself too. Since my father's death she hadn't said it once.

I knew that it would be best to wait before asking whether I could go to Cascina Marchesini that Saturday and I was particularly helpful that evening – so helpful, in fact, that my mother scolded me for fussing and getting in her way.

I saw Gianfrancesco the following day in the schoolyard. He was standing alone, leaning against the wall of the sports hall. Rita did not want to go over with me to talk to him.

'My father says his mother's a Fascist,' she said. 'You go and talk to him if you want. I'm not coming.'

Gianfrancesco looked pleased when he saw me. He said immediately, 'Did you ask your mother whether you could come to my house?'

'Not yet.'

'Will you ask her?'

I nodded, but perhaps he had noticed the doubt on my face.

'Don't forget to tell her about the pears.'

When I asked my mother that evening, she wasn't keen to allow me to go. She listed the chores which I needed to do before she would consider it, and the list was quite a comprehensive one.

However, the mention of a bounty of fruit was enough to soften her resistance eventually. She told me to ride my bicycle carefully, to pull over and stop if I heard a car and be home by five o'clock.

Zia Mina had procured a bicycle for me. I think she hoped it would provide some distraction following my father's death. Salvatore had taught me to ride it in the yard. I loved it and happily volunteered to ride to the village to carry out small errands whenever I could. I didn't tell Zia Mina where I was going that afternoon.

It was a beautiful, hazy, late-September day. The summer heat had abated, the mosquitoes had died off and the leaves on the trees rattled gently as they dried out and prepared to fall.

I had never been on the North Road alone before. I had ridden out in the other direction to go to the village, but never on the North Road. There had been no reason for me to do so. I had a sense of freedom, as though I could ride on for ever. I held my breath as I cycled across the canal.

Gianfrancesco was sitting on the grass verge, his back against one of the brick gateposts. He leaped to his feet and waved when he saw me.

'I'm so glad you've come,' he called out, smiling broadly. 'Your mother didn't mind?'

'I had to do a lot of jobs first.'

'And I had homework to do.'

His bicycle, which was enormous, was propped against the other post.

'Can you actually ride that big machine?' I asked.

'More or less. It was my father's and I still need to grow into it; plus I need some speed to get it going and then jump on. It's a technique.' He held up a grazed elbow. 'A technique I have yet to perfect.'

I looked at the old gateposts, which still seemed nonsensical to me and asked, 'Were there walls or hedges here once?'

'No.'

'Then what's the point of having gates?'

'There used to be deep ditches. They were to keep cows in, not people out,' he said, then looked sadly across the fields. 'But there are no cows to keep in now.'

'What happened to them? You had three hundred of them, you told me before.'

'They were sold. After my father died, Mamma thought she could employ somebody to look after them, but it wasn't possible. They had debts, you see.'

'The cows had debts?'

'No, silly.' He laughed. 'My parents were the ones with the debts.'

The farm was silent. All the barn doors were closed. Patches of weeds grew in stringy tufts. There was a mournful, neglected feeling to the place. A small, solitary grey hen picked at the cracked ground.

The huge wedding-cake house had all its shutters drawn. The oleanders looked shrunken and close to death. I stopped and pointed at the coat of arms above the central window.

'Are those herons?'

'Yes,' he replied. 'I'm surprised you can make them out. The carving's quite badly eroded.'

'I saw them in your family mausoleum. My father said he thought they had a meaning.'

'They do. Several meanings, actually. In Ancient Greece the heron was the symbol of the struggle of good overpowering evil. It has other meanings too, like peace and longevity. And of course here in this region herons were really common. Not so much now the rice fields are gone, but we do still see them along the rivers. On our coat of arms their necks make the shape of an M for Marchesini. And some people say we look like herons because we've all got long legs, but I don't think that was intentional when the coat of arms was designed though.' He smiled.

'That's funny. When my aunt worked in the rice fields they used to call her "The Heron" because she was so tall.'

We made our way around the side. The only sign of life was an assortment of tattered dishrags drying on a wooden stand. Suddenly Gianfrancesco stopped and said, 'Do you miss your father a lot?'

'Yes.'

'I miss mine a lot too. But it gets better with time. Whenever I think of him, I try to remember all the nice times we had together. Like being out in the fields, or on the tractor with him, or in his study looking at his books. It helps. I call it making a stone memory.'

'A stone memory?'

Gianfrancesco nodded. 'I read that memories can be like pictures drawn in sand. A gust of wind can blow them away and they can be gone and forgotten forever. So I imagine that all the good times with my father are carved into stone. I think of them over and over again until I'm certain of every detail, and as I'm thinking, I imagine those details chiselled into stone so that I can remember them forever.'

'I like that. I'm going to do that too.'

'And thankfully I have some photographs. Do you have photographs of your father?'

'No,' I replied sadly. 'We didn't even have one to put on his tomb.'

Gianfrancesco said quietly, 'My mother is very different now. Is yours?'

'Yes. She's stricter. She gets impatient more easily. I think she misses Papá a lot, but I also think she's relieved he doesn't feel any more pain.'

'My mother was hysterical. A doctor had to give her an injection to calm her and now she has to take pills to sleep. But don't tell anyone that. She wouldn't want anybody to know.'

I bowed my head. Suddenly it felt very heavy.

'Are you afraid you'll lose her too?' I mumbled.

'Sometimes I can't sleep for worrying about it,' Gianfrancesco confessed. 'Even though I know it's very unlikely, I imagine her having an accident in the car, or taking too many pills and never waking up.'

'I feel exactly the same as you. I think about terrible things happening and of being left all by myself.' I looked up, expecting Gianfrancesco to appear gloomy, but all I could see in his expression was relief.

'I'm glad it's not just me,' he said.

We spent the afternoon wandering around Cascina Marchesini, exploring its abandoned barns and outbuildings. The dairy was locked shut, its windows obscured by cobwebs. The milking machines stood silent. The cheese store was empty.

But as we meandered through the orchards, chatting and picking pears I felt happier than I had since Papá had died.

'Take as many pears as you want,' Gianfrancesco told me. 'I'm afraid they will go to waste otherwise.'

'You can preserve them. You shouldn't waste food.'

'I know. But my mother isn't interested in things like that and Fiorella has so much to do, she wouldn't have time.'

'We could do it,' I suggested. 'If we had sugar and jars.'

'Do you know how?'

'Yes, of course. I've seen my aunt do it loads of times. Pears, peaches, cherries, plums. You can preserve anything in sugar. Would your mother let us?'

'I don't see why not. I would have to ask first, but she doesn't usually mind what I do as long as I'm here and I've done my homework. How about your mother? She could have some of the preserved fruit, of course. She could have half of it. And your aunt. She could have some too.'

We both grinned excitedly. Gianfrancesco clapped his hands together.

'A project!' he announced. 'It's great to have a project.'

'We will need sugar though, quite a lot of it. And a lemon, maybe several lemons. And we have to sterilise the jars or the fruit could go fizzy and make us ill.'

'We need a list then. Wait here.' He ran fast back to the house and returned a short time later with a jotter and pencil. 'Right,' he said breathlessly. 'You're the expert here. What's the first thing we need?'

'We need to harvest the fruit.'

'Of course.' He noted this down. I saw that his handwriting was beautiful. 'Then what?'

'We have to get the jars ready. That will take some time. You see, we have to put them in boiling water to sterilise them, then let them cool. I will have to see what kind of jars you have. Are they the ones with rubber seals?'

Gianfrancesco shrugged. 'I don't know, but I can show you.'

I was enjoying the feeling of being an expert.

'If they are, we might need new rubber seals. If we can't get them we can use some paraffin wax.'

'Come and see,' he said.

We made our way to the house, chattering excitedly about our project. Gianfrancesco asked more questions than I knew how to answer, but I promised that I would consult my aunt about anything that was uncertain.

The kitchen was no different to the way I remembered it. Spinning blizzards of dust caught in the smoky light. Gianfrancesco led me through to a back kitchen, and through again to a store room.

I had been expecting to see a few jars, perhaps a few dozen or so. So I was astounded to see shelf after shelf of empty glass jars, vessels and pots rising from floor to ceiling. They were covered in a thick layer of dust. It was a sight that would have sent my aunt into a frenzy. She was always short of jars.

'They haven't been used for years,' said Gianfrancesco. 'Not since long before my father died.'

We spent an hour sorting through the most appropriate containers. We carried the best of them to the kitchen and set them out on the table. The array was quite daunting.

'It's going to be a long day's work,' I said. I sounded like my aunt.

During the following week of school we spent every moment of our break-times planning. Gianfrancesco noted everything down in his jotter. His mother had given permission for us to carry out our pear project, albeit reluctantly at first. My mother took a little more convincing, but I knew that the promise of pears would be enough to gain her approval in the end.

The following Saturday I arrived at Cascina Marchesini at 8 a.m. sharp.

The kitchen stove was enormous, just like everything else in the house. It was four times the size of ours and sat within a deep stone fireplace. As directed, Gianfrancesco had filled several saucepans with water, which were already simmering when I arrived. He had washed the dust off the jars and lined them up on the table ready for sterilisation. The shards of light which squeezed through the gaps in the louvres hit the glass, bouncing half-moons of coloured rainbows against the walls. A pile of clean cloths was set neatly beside them.

'Right!' he said, rubbing his hands together. 'You're the expert here. You direct me.'

I had brought along one of my mother's aprons, which I felt gave me an added air of professionalism. I was the expert, after all. I wanted to look the part. As soon as he saw me put it on, Gianfrancesco went to find something similar. I had never seen a boy in an apron before. His long skinny legs and big-booted feet stuck out underneath. It made me laugh.

'What do you think?' He posed, spinning around and grinning. 'It's Fiorella's apron, but I don't think she'll mind.'

I checked the water on the stove, which was starting to boil.

'It's ready,' I said. 'We need to put a cloth in the bottom of each pan to protect the glass.'

Carefully, we began to transfer the jars into the saucepans.

'How long do they need?' asked Gianfrancesco.

'About twenty minutes. We can start peeling the pears in the meantime.'

It soon became clear that I was rather more experienced at fruit-peeling than he was. I had helped my aunt and my mother prepare fruit so often that with a single incision of my knife and the careful turning of the fruit in my hand I could remove the skin in a single, elegant coil. Gianfrancesco fumbled with the knife, hacking off little chunks and far too much pear with the peel.

'Use your knife more lightly,' I advised. 'You're wasting a lot of fruit.'

He stabbed at his pear and laughed as I produced yet another graceful spiral of skin.

By the time the jars had boiled sufficiently, we had a good amount of fruit prepared. We carefully set the jars to cool on the side.

Gianfrancesco had procured the largest sack of sugar I had ever seen. It was so heavy he had to drag it across the floor.

'Where on earth did you get that?' I asked.

'From the bakery in Mazzolo. I swapped it for three chairs. But my mother doesn't know.'

'You swapped it for three chairs?' I was amazed.

He nodded. 'The chapel's full of chairs. I don't think they'll be missed. The baker even gave me lemons and asked if we were going to use cinnamon or nutmeg. I didn't know but I took the cinnamon and nutmeg anyway.'

'That's enough for a massive amount of pears,' I noted, looking at it all.

'Perfect, because we do have a massive amount of pears. And we also have a massive number of jars.'

'Maybe we should just start with what we've got here.'

'Yes. Best to do things properly in smaller amounts.'

We set two of the saucepans back onto the stove, filled them with the appropriate amounts of water, sugar and lemon juice, and weighed out peeled and quartered pears.

Once the sugar water was simmering, we added the fruit. It was almost one o'clock by the time we were ready to place our mixture into the jars. The kitchen was filled with the most heavenly scent.

It took us over an hour to transfer all of our delectable concoction into the jars. By the time we had finished, we had twenty-four jars of preserved pears. A bowlful was left, which we agreed would make an excellent lunch.

'This is the best thing I've done for ages,' Gianfrancesco said, as we sat on the kitchen steps, sharing from the same bowl.

'Me too,' I replied, grinning.

We dug at the pears in the bowl, chasing the last few chunks with our forks. By the time we had drunk the juice we both felt quite sick.

'Where's your mother?' I asked. I had expected Signora Marchesini to appear at some stage. I was curious to see what she might be wearing.

'She goes to Cremona to have lunch with a friend and do some shopping most Saturdays,' Gianfrancesco replied. Suddenly a quizzical look spread across his face.

'I've just thought: how are you going to carry the jars home on your bicycle?' he asked. This aspect had not crossed my mind.

'I don't know. Perhaps you could lend me a basket to hang on my handlebars?'

'I could. But you will only be able to take a few jars. Half are for you.'

'I don't have to take them all at the same time. Anyway, half is a lot. They're your pears and you paid for the sugar and lemons.'

'The chairs paid for the sugar and lemons. But your expertise was invaluable.'

I frowned in thought. 'I will have to make a few trips,' I said.

'I can ride back to your house with you I can take some on my father's bicycle too.'

'Could you do it without falling off?' I was doubtful. 'Your feet don't reach the ground.'

'It would be risky.'

'We can't risk smashing the jars after all that work.'

'How about you take one or two jars now and I bring another to school every day for you? You can carry one jar home easily.'

We agreed that this would be the best plan. We cleared up the kitchen, took a bucket of fruit peel to the chickens and I prepared to make my way home.

I wheeled off happily down the avenue, a jar of pears tied to each side of my handlebars. I had wrapped them in cloths and bound them with string. Gianfrancesco had been impressed by my ingenuity. I sang to myself as I pedalled along, breathing in the balmy late-afternoon air, and promised that I'd re-live the day in my thoughts over and over again so that I would never forget it. I would make a stone memory.

I was almost home when I was winded by a stabbing pain in my belly. It hurt so much I had to stop, but I could not get off my bicycle as I was paralysed by cramp. A clammy chill rose through me and I thought I would be sick, or soil myself, or both. My palms were sweating.

Somehow I managed to get off my bicycle and lay it on the verge, careful not to damage the jars of pears.

There is no pleasant way to describe what happened next. I was overwhelmed by the need to empty my bowels, and the only place I could do it was in the ditch by the roadside. I squatted there nervously, praying that nobody would pass by. I was obliged to leave my fouled underwear in the ditch. At a rough estimate, I had eaten about ten stewed pears that day for lunch. Their laxative effect had been devastating.

My mother was delighted with the pears, although she did suggest that next time we should shorten the cooking time slightly so the fruit would remain firmer. I thought that Zia Mina would be pleased too, but when I presented her with our creation she said, 'I've enough preserved fruit of my own. I don't need the Marchesinis' charity.'

As agreed, Gianfrancesco brought a jar of pears to school every day for me to take home. Every break-time, as before, we would meet in the yard and discuss our project.

Rita was not pleased with me. She did not like sharing me with Gianfrancesco. She had made new friends in her class and preferred to sit and chat with them at break-time.

On Friday I looked around the yard for Gianfrancesco. He was not in his usual spot by the wall. I waited through most of break-time, but he did not appear. It was only when I heard shouting from the toilet block at the far end of the yard that I spotted him. He was surrounded by a group of boys who were trying to wrestle his satchel from him. It had come undone in the struggle. There were books, papers and pencils on the ground. One of the boys was holding up a jar of pears.

I ran over as fast as I could, shouting at them to stop. The two who noticed me seemed surprised that a small First-Year girl like me would try to intervene. The boys were older than me, some by five years. They were still in middle school because they had failed their end-of-year exams more than once and had to repeat the whole school year each time. They had out-grown middle school physically, but not academically. Although he was tall for his age, Gianfrancesco was not as thickset as his aggressors, and he was seriously outnumbered.

I flew into the tussle, using my elbows to great effect. The boys backed off more out of surprise than anything else. Gianfrancesco had been pushed to the ground and was clutching his bag tightly against his body, partly to save its contents and partly to protect himself from the kicking which was about to take place.

'You stay away!' I screamed. 'Stay away!'

I stood squarely between the boys and Gianfrancesco.

'Why? What are you going to do, little girl?' sneered one.

'Marchesini needs a girl to protect him!' jeered another. 'Maybe she needs to learn a lesson as well.' He reached out and took hold of my hair. He tugged so hard it hurt my neck and I was immobilised. He shook me, then amused himself leading me like a haltered mule in circles around where he was standing.

Gianfrancesco scrambled to get up, shouting at them to let me go, but two boys pinned him down.

'See this, Marchesini? Your little girlie friend ain't much good to you now, is she? Look at her – she'll do anything I say. Kneel down, little girl!' With that, he wrenched my head again so that I had no choice but to drop to my knees. The sharp gravel of the yard cut into my kneecaps.

'You can get a girl to suck your dick when she's on her knees,' said the boy. 'Shall we try it? Do you want to watch your little girlie friend suck my dick, Marchesini? I bet you wish she was sucking yours.' His grip tightened. 'No, wait, I don't suppose you've got one, have you?'

They all laughed. I knelt contorted on the ground. He brought his face close to mine.

'You want to taste some dick?' He smirked, yanking at my hair in such a way as to make me nod. 'Look, Marchesini! Yes, she does. She really, really wants it!'

As he tugged on my hair again, forcing me to nod, I felt my fist fly into his face. The arc of my outstretched arm delivered a single, precise blow. It could not have been a luckier punch. The crack of his nose breaking as it made contact with my knuckles seemed to reverberate through the schoolyard. He yelped and let go of my hair immediately.

There was a loud gasp and much shouting from the rabble which had gathered around us to watch the affray. The boy howled, cupping his broken and bleeding nose in his hands. His friends let go of Gianfrancesco, who stood up shakily.

The commotion had attracted the attention of the headmaster, who pushed his way through the crowd demanding to know what was going on.

As we all stood lined up in the headmaster's office, the boys pleaded innocence and misunderstanding – but it seemed that the headmaster had heard it all before.

The boy whose nose I had broken was called Bruno. He was holding a bloodied handkerchief to his face. Bruising was starting to bloom under his eyes.

'Would you care to explain what happened?' asked the headmaster.

'We were just messing about,' said Bruno with some difficulty through his handkerchief. 'Just having a laugh with Marchesini. Weren't we, Marchesini?'

The other boys made noises of agreement, though Gianfrancesco did not. The headmaster raised an eyebrow doubtfully.

'No, sir,' said Gianfrancesco firmly. He looked pale. His glasses sat slightly twisted. 'I was in the cloakroom when they came in and grabbed my satchel. They put my history notes down the lavatory and tore up my maths book. And then they threatened to smash my jar of pears.'

The boys made noises of shock and denial, but Gianfrancesco continued to explain.

'And when I tried to get away, they chased me into the yard and pushed me over. It was then that Graziella came to try to stop them. None of this is her fault. Please don't punish her, sir.'

'She broke Bruno's nose!' exclaimed one of the boys indignantly.

The headmaster looked me up and down. I was significantly smaller than anyone else in the line.

'It was *you* who broke Bruno's nose?' he asked with some surprise.

I nodded.

'Sir, she had no choice. Please don't punish her,' Gianfrancesco pleaded again. 'He grabbed her hair and threatened her.'

'He threatened her?'

'Yes, sir. Graziella only wanted to help me. he asked them to leave me alone, but Bruno took her by the hair and…' Gianfrancesco swallowed hard.

'And what?'

My friend seemed to be searching for his words. 'He threatened to make her…'

'Make her do what? Come on boy, spit it out!'

'He threatened to make her perform a sexual act. A disgusting sexual act. He made the threat repeatedly and in the coarsest language.'

The headmaster turned to Bruno.

'Is that the case?' he demanded. Bruno and his accomplices protested innocence.

The headmaster turned back to Gianfrancesco.

'That is a weighty accusation,' he said. 'Can you tell me exactly what was threatened?'

Gianfrancesco looked at me, then back at the headmaster and stood up as straight as he could.

'I cannot, sir,' he said firmly. 'I cannot let Graziella hear it again. But there were many witnesses who would have heard it.'

The witnesses were called and each corroborated the evidence given. Gianfrancesco and I were dismissed without punishment.

Both my mother and Signora Marchesini were summoned to

school separately. My mother was not angry with me, but instead expressed concern at the fact that I had placed myself in a dangerous situation.

Signora Marchesini, on the other hand, insisted that the school must punish Bruno and his gang. There must be consequences to their actions, she said firmly. They spent the remainder of the term raking leaves and picking litter from the yard every break-time and cleaning the lavatories after school.

They never bothered me or Gianfrancesco again.

CHAPTER 15

I found my schoolwork very difficult. The jump from elementary school to middle school was enormous. I was overwhelmed by the different subjects. I longed to sing my times tables, write stories, learn poems and draw pictures, but the time for such childish learning had passed.

Gianfrancesco was right. Time did lessen the grief I felt for the loss of my father, and the fear of losing my mother in some tragic way had also diminished, but my mind still did not seem able to focus. I would listen in class, take notes and by the time I returned home and opened my books to do my homework, whatever knowledge had been imparted to me that day had dissolved away.

It was the last day of school before the Christmas break and I had been given my report. The rule was that it should be opened by parents, but unable to stand the wait, I tore open the envelope at school.

My grades were not good. Each subject was graded from zero to ten. My report card showed a list of threes, fours and fives. If I did not improve each one to at least a six, I would have to repeat the year, just like the big, stupid boys who had bullied Gianfrancesco.

I cried hard. I was going to fail school.

'What's happened?' Gianfrancesco said, dropping his bag.

I could say nothing. I could only shake my head and sob. I passed my report to him.

'This is quite poor,' he said. 'You will have to repeat the year if you don't raise your grades.'

Stating such an obvious thing did not help at all and made me cry even harder. He placed a comforting hand on my shoulder.

'Don't cry, Graziella. It's not the end of the world. You still have two whole terms to bring these grades up to scratch and I can help you if you would like me to. We can study together through the holidays.'

The days before Christmas were bitterly cold. Sharp sleet fell and iced the roads, and quickly turned to snow, which settled thickly, obliterating the distinction between roads and fields, smothering boundaries and turning the world around Paradiso into a single bleak, white mass. The sound of the church bell, which normally rang clearly every hour, was distorted to a muffled clang.

Gutters groaned and bowed with the weight of the snow. The creamy yellow buildings in the village faded into the whiteness until all that was visible was a bloom of orange tiles around each smoking chimney.

The cold forced its way into the house. We stuffed rags and newspaper between the windows and the shutters, and even into the keyhole, but still the cold broke in. No matter how much we fed the stove, it seemed to become hungrier, gobbling quantities of wood which worried my mother. Running the stove too hot could crack the fire box.

I would check the temperature by spitting on the cast-iron slab. My saliva had to fizz and skip across the hotplate. If it exploded and vanished instantly, the stove was too hot and the firebox had to be opened, but this used more wood.

I looked out across the snowy yard and thought that there was little hope of Gianfrancesco coming to help with my studies; but he arrived at Paradiso as promised, wearing an enormous sheepskin jacket and fur hat which had belonged to his father. It had taken him almost three hours to walk here from Cascina Marchesini.

Despite his warm clothing, he was half-frozen. My mother said he had been foolish to walk out on such a foul day. She took his wet clothes and boots and lent him a pair of my father's old trousers and a woollen waistcoat to wear, then made him sit by the stove and gave him hot soup. When he asked for a spoon, she told him to hold the bowl in his hands to warm them and to drink from it directly. He seemed to find such rustic manners quite charming, but declared soon after finishing the soup that he had thawed and that he was ready to settle down to work.

He looked odd, bizarrely dressed in a combination of both our dead fathers' clothes, but had an air of purpose as he spread his books out on the table.

'I am your tutor today, not just your friend,' he began. 'We are going to start with literature. You will be studying this after Christmas. It is *The Betrothed* by Alessandro Manzoni.'

He took out a red velvet case, embroidered with a splendid gold shield. Inside was a large tome, bound in white leather with silver embossed writing on the cover.

'This was my father's copy. It's an illustrated limited edition print from 1904. It's extremely valuable so we have to be very careful with it. Please don't bend the spine.'

I looked at the huge book. I couldn't imagine myself reading something so weighty. My trepidation was confirmed when Gianfrancesco told me that it had originally been published in three volumes and had taken Alessandro Manzoni seventeen years to write. I feared it might take me a similar length of time to read it.

'When studying any work of literature you must read it with several things in mind,' said Gianfrancesco. His tone was serious. 'You must consider the characters, the context, the themes and the message the book is trying to convey. Once you have a good idea of those, you can begin to look more deeply into the way it is written, the use of language, and begin to formulate your own opinions. Parallel to this, you must know something about the author.'

It all seemed so far beyond me. All I could do was to stare at the silver writing.

'So, we are going to start by reading it,' he began. 'We'll take turns. One page each. We will stop whenever there is anything worthy of discussion.'

'Have you read it before?'

'Of course. I've read it four times. This will be my fifth study of it and each time I read it, I learn something new from it.'

I was overwhelmed by the reading aloud. The language was difficult. Often I found myself distracted by the beautiful illustrations. At the beginning of every chapter there was a detailed engraving, depicting the characters and the landscape.

Gianfrancesco stopped reading, placed his bookmark on the last line we had read and asked, 'What is the purpose of studying literature?' He was looking at me intently over the rim of his spectacles.

'To improve our reading?'

'Well, reading will improve with practice, yes. But what is the purpose of *really* reading and trying to understand what the author is trying to say?'

'I don't know.'

'It is to train our minds to think more deeply about all matters in our lives,' he said. '*The Betrothed* is a very important work of Italian literature. Some people say that it is *the* most important work. There are many reasons for which it is important. Firstly, it deals with a number of very significant themes, such as good versus evil, power, greed and love. We can learn a lot about human nature from it. It asks a lot of questions which make us think about ourselves and how we treat others.'

I was entranced by Gianfrancesco's words.

'Some of the locations are quite close to here,' he continued, then cleared his throat. 'My father promised he would take me on a tour of those places, but we only got the chance to go to Lake Como.'

We resumed taking turns reading. Gianfrancesco read better

than I did and with more expression and fluency than any teacher I had ever heard read. At times I was so mesmerised that I would beg him to read on a little further, but he was strict, making me read every other page, as we had agreed at the start.

The more I read the more my reading improved, and by chapter four I was gaining some of Gianfrancesco's expressive skill.

The story involved Renzo and Lucia, two young lovers from a village in Lombardy. My mind began to wander. I tried to picture Pieve Santa Clara as it would have been in the seventeenth century and I dreamed that the two young lovers were Gianfrancesco and myself. I wondered whether he was thinking the same.

Renzo and Lucia planned to marry, but an evil nobleman wanted Lucia for himself and forbade the priest from performing the ceremony.

'What do we learn about power here?' asked Gianfrancesco.

'That a nobleman is more powerful than a priest?'

'Yes! Good! And what else do we learn?'

'That Renzo loves Lucia.'

'Yes. We also learn how difficult it can be to speak the truth. It's not the priest's fault that he cannot marry Renzo and Lucia, but he does not have the courage to tell either of them. How does Manzoni make us feel sympathy for the priest?'

'There's nothing he can do, so we feel sorry for him.'

'Yes, but what device does Manzoni use to express this more fully?'

'Device?'

'He uses humour. He uses irony and sarcasm and makes us feel pity towards him. All those things are devices used in literature. A device is like a tool for a writer. Just as a carpenter uses a plane or a saw a writer uses irony, or humour, or emotive language.'

By the time we reached chapter nine Lucia had escaped to a convent to hide from the nobleman, but in hiding there, she had to take vows of chastity and renounce Renzo.

'What's the point of that?' I asked. 'She wants to marry, so she goes into hiding, but the place she hides is one where she has to renounce marriage. It makes no sense!'

'It's a paradox.'

'What's a paradox?'

'It's a contradiction, an impossible circumstance.'

I had hoped for an uplifting love story, but the romance was obscured by strife. Love seemed hopeless and unreachable.

'It's quite miserable. Everything is so hard for Renzo and Lucia. All they wanted to do was to get married,' I said. I was no longer imagining Gianfrancesco and myself as the lovers. The whole thing was too impossibly complex.

'Yes, but this is more than just a love story. What good would a book be if two people who wanted to get married just got married and lived happily ever after?'

'I think I would like a book like that.'

'Nobody would read a book if it didn't contain intrigue or struggle. Good literature makes us think. And the subject of love is fertile ground for any writer. Some of the greatest works of literature are about love and they contain great literary characters. Romeo and Juliet, for example, or Paolo and Francesca.'

'Did Romeo and Juliet get married?'

'Yes, but they killed themselves shortly afterwards.'

'And Paolo and Francesca?'

'No. They were punished for eternity in hell for adultery.'

It seemed that every word which left Gianfrancesco's lips taught me something, or made me think. He had read more books by the age of fifteen than I thought it would be possible to read in a lifetime.

By the end of the lesson my head was spinning and I was so tired that I felt as though my brain had been wrung out. I was overwhelmed with the feeling of having been thoroughly educated.

'I have to go home,' said Gianfrancesco finally.

'Not in this weather, surely? It'll be dark soon,' said my mother.

'My mother will worry, Signora Ponti.'

'She's probably already worried. You should never have come all this way on a day like this.'

Gianfrancesco peered out of the window. 'Thank you for your concern, but it's all right, Signora Ponti. The clouds have cleared. It's going to get colder, but it won't snow again tonight.'

As Gianfrancesco had forecast, it did not snow again, but it became even colder. The night sky was clear and mauve and scattered with stars. The metre of snow which had settled during the day froze to a glittering, crystallised mass. My mother and I both slept in the bed in the kitchen that night under a pile of blankets and we each wore a pair of my father's socks.

By the morning, trees dripped with icy spikes. Sharp spears hung from our eaves and clung to the wires of fences. Everything was rendered rigid with ice.

The electricity went off and did not come back on again for three days. We ran out of candles and had to improvise by lighting oily rags in jars. The smell and the black fug which smouldered from them reminded me of Ernesto.

Still, Gianfrancesco came every day. He said that the five-hour return journey did not bother him and that spending four hours in our warm kitchen was delightful.

'It's so cold at my house that we have ice on the *inside* of the windows,' he said.

We started reading three days before Christmas Eve, and by the Feast of Epiphany, we had finished. Following all manner of misfortunes, including surviving war and famine and contracting the plague, Renzo and Lucia were married.

*

At the beginning of term, I returned to school with a new sense of purpose. Gianfrancesco had not just taught me facts, he had taught me how to think about what I was learning. It was as though his intelligence had infected me.

We were inseparable through our break-times and we met every Saturday and most Sundays to study together. I had convinced him to start taking the school bus. I would always reserve a seat next to me as Gianfrancesco's stop was after mine on the way in. The boys who had taunted him left him alone. I had been congratulated by numerous children for having subdued Bruno the bully, whose nose had never looked quite the same again.

As spring bloomed and the days lengthened, so did our time spent studying together. I would do my chores every Saturday morning and after lunch I would ride over to Gianfrancesco's. We would study for as long as we could as we had to leave time for me to return home before it got dark. He would go through the previous week's work methodically, testing me with questions and often expanding the topic by teaching me things the teacher had not covered. He would then oversee my homework. Thanks to his help, my grades improved weekly.

My mother liked Gianfrancesco and was grateful that he was helping me with my studies. Zia Mina, on the other hand, was displeased that I spent so much time at Cascina Marchesini. I think she had quarrelled with my mother about it, but the improvement in my grades and my new lust for learning overrode her disapproval.

Rita was not impressed, even though she had new friends. One Saturday she was sitting outside her house, bouncing the pram which contained yet another baby sibling. One of her new friends from school was sitting with her.

'Going to see Gianfrancesco?' she called out in a sing-song voice.

I nodded. The two girls turned towards each other, whispered and giggled.

'Are you going to kiss him?' asked Rita's friend. They burst into peals of laughter.

'No, I am not!' I protested, then got on my bicycle and sped off down the road, fuming with indignation.

The fact was that I wished I *could* kiss Gianfrancesco. It was something I thought about all the time. If I did, what would he do? Would he kiss me back, or would he jump away in horror? And how would I do it? He was quite a bit taller than me. We would have to be sitting down.

Sometimes as we sat together poring over texts, our faces so close that we could feel each other's breath, I would lose myself so completely in the thought of kissing him that I would forget what I was supposed to be studying.

I was madly, passionately and secretly in love.

*

On the last day before the summer break, I was handed my report. Each of my grades had risen by at least three points. I had achieved a nine for literature, thanks in part to the essay I had written discussing humour, power and paradoxes in Alessandro Manzoni's *The Betrothed*. My teacher had noted that I had an 'insightful approach'. Best of all, I was top of the class.

I showed my report to Gianfrancesco.

He was pleased. 'That's better. And I can still help you to improve.'

'It's all thanks to you,' I said, and quite spontaneously I did that thing I had been thinking about ceaselessly. I kissed Gianfrancesco. It was not a tentative peck, but a heartfelt kiss, delivered directly on his unsuspecting mouth.

For a moment he seemed disorientated, then he grinned, grasped my face in his hands and kissed me back, saying in a slightly breathless way, 'You're welcome!'

From that moment on we spent almost as much time kissing as we did studying.

It might seem fanciful to say that a thirteen-year-old girl and a fifteen-year-old boy could be truly in love, but we were. Whenever I thought of Gianfrancesco, which was most of the time, a delicious warmth would bubble though me; and when we were together, that fizzing feeling would fill me to the point where I thought I would burst. Gianfrancesco felt it too.

As I pushed open the gate and made my way across the yard towards Paradiso with my report card in my hand, a sense of excitement for things to come overwhelmed me.

My mother was at the door watching my approach. It was unusual for her to be waiting for me like that; she had been so cold and distant since my father's death. But as she stood on the doorstep beside the missing brick, squinting at the sunshine, I could see that she was smiling.

She read my report in silence, then held it up with the written side facing the sky and called out, 'Look! Look, Luigi! You see what a clever girl your daughter is?'

With that my mother pulled me into her arms and hugged me tightly.

'You're a good girl,' she said. 'Everything's going to be all right.'

Acknowledgements

With thanks to my husband, Chris Lowe, and to my children Jake and Nellie Lowe for your unwavering patience, support and belief.

To my parents – Victoria Scanacapra for your cultural input and historical recollections, and Valerio Scanacapra for your advice concerning all things mechanical.

To my uncle, Frank Constable, for being my number one reader.

And to the late Roger Tallack, my brilliant English teacher, who predicted that one day I would write a book.

Return to Paradiso, the sequel to *Paradiso*
is available now:

Italy, 1950. The dawn of a new decade brings with it the promise
of lasting peace and prosperity as the hardships of war are
consigned to the past.

In Pieve Santa Clara, a tiny village in rural Lombardy, Graziella
Ponti, now a teenager, lives a simple life with her widowed mother
and aunt.

But Italy is transforming around Graziella at great speed and,
as her childhood gives way to the start of her womanhood, she
must learn to navigate this ever-changing new world.

Return to Paradiso is a story of love, hope and tragedy set in Italy
at a time when the Economic Miracle is in full swing, the grip of
the Catholic Church is loosening, and the role of women in
society is making significant progress.

The second of the ***Paradiso Novels***, this is a compelling and
emotionally-charged historical novel perfect for fans of Dinah
Jeffries, Lucinda Riley, Angela Petch and Victoria Hislop.

For more information, find both books at Amazon or visit
www.silvertailbooks.com.

Printed in Great Britain
by Amazon